To my niece and nephew, Chantelle and Eytan,
and to all the people you might become

WHEN I WAS ME

WHEN I WAS ME

HILARY FREEMAN

HOT
KEY
BOOKS

First published in Great Britain in 2015 by Hot Key Books
Northburgh House, 10 Northburgh Street, London EC1V 0AT

A CIP catalogue record for this book is available from the British Library.

ISBN: 978-1-4714-0492-4

1

This book is typeset in 11pt Sabon using Atomik ePublisher

Printed and bound by Clays Ltd, St Ives Plc

www.hotkeybooks.com

Hot Key Books is part of the Bonnier Publishing Group
www.bonnierpublishing.com

The display says there's a five-minute wait for my bus, so I perch on the plastic bench, next to a young woman who is talking on her mobile phone. After a minute or so, we're joined by an old lady, her shoulders draped in a bright red knitted shawl. She is hunched over a trolley, which she is half pushing, half leaning on, and walking so slowly that each step seems to be a monumental effort. I stand up so that she can sit down in my place but, instead of taking my seat, she backs away. Then she stares at me, with eyes so pale and cloudy that they're almost translucent, her gaze so hard and cold it feels like it's boring right through me. It makes me shudder. Not knowing how to react, I turn away, pretending to read the bus timetable.

'It's you!' she declares. 'You!'

I smile nervously, and edge towards her. 'What did you say?'

'You! I know you.' She doesn't say it in a pleasant, friendly way. It sounds more like an accusation.

1

'I'm sorry? You must be mistaken . . .' I look over to the young woman for support, but she's still engrossed in her conversation and either hasn't heard what's going on, or is pretending that nothing is happening.

'I know you,' says the old lady again.

'No, I don't think so. Maybe you've just seen me at this bus stop before. Or maybe you're confusing me with someone else.'

She shakes her head, reaching down to move her trolley closer to her, as if she thinks I might steal it. A gnarled, arthritic finger reaches out towards me and wavers millimetres from my chest. 'I know you. I know who you are. I know what you are. You're dangerous. Keep away, I tell you. Don't touch me.'

Unnerved, I again appeal to the young woman with my eyes, but she just looks down, as if I'm disturbing her.

'Don't come near me . . . Don't touch me. Do you hear me? Leave me alone!'

'I'm not going to do anything . . .' I begin, but the old woman has already begun to shuffle off, taking her possessions with her. When she reaches the end of the bus stop she turns. 'Don't come after me! Do you hear? Go away!'

'I'm not going to hurt you . . . You've got the wrong person . . .'

Now the young woman is looking at me and shaking her head. She tuts. 'Weirdo.'

'Yes, really creepy,' I say, forcing a laugh. But I don't feel like laughing; I feel frightened. I feel exposed. Who is this

2

old woman and what does she think that I've done? Her words ring in my ears: 'I know you.' Something tells me that she is not just a batty old lady; she truly does know who I am – the real me. I sense that she can see me in a way that no one else can. She seems aware that something isn't right with me, and recognises that I'm only pretending to be like everybody else. And maybe she knows the truth about what has happened to me.

1

Awakening

Something isn't right.

My eyes are still only half open but I can already tell that I'm not where I'm supposed to be. The light seeping into the room is too warm, its glow too pink, and when I roll over on to my right side I find myself pressing up against a solid wall. A wall that shouldn't be there.

Confused, I grasp for my bedside light switch but I can't find it; I can't even find the bedside table, which appears to have moved away in the night. It must be somewhere nearby because I can hear the sound of my clock radio, and a voice I don't recognise announcing that it's seven o'clock on Monday morning. Seven a.m.: the time I need to get up for college. That, at least, is as it should be.

But everything else is wrong. I can't blame my eyes because now they're fully open, the sleep rubbed away, and I've widened and shut them and widened and shut them enough times to know that they're working properly. I feel

4

disoriented, like you do when you stay at a friend's house and wake up in the morning, and for a moment forget where you have spent the night. But that feeling always passes in an instant, and this feeling, this sense of unease, is growing, as everything I see becomes more unfamiliar and more weird.

I drag myself up and sit on the edge of the bed, trying to take in what's around me. The shape of this room is like mine, its size the same, the door and the window in the same positions. It's the details that are wrong, the furniture and the colours, the way that everything is decorated and arranged.

I am certain I did not stay at anyone else's house. I remember going to bed last night in my own home, in my own room, in my own bed. I remember tucking myself in to my duvet, and turning off my bedside light. It was midnight. I remember checking my phone three times before I went to sleep, to see if there were any texts. There were none. Then I left the phone under the pillow, like I always do. And now I can't feel it there. It's gone.

My bed is in the wrong place, pushed up against the wall, when it should be in the centre of the room, facing out towards the window. The duvet I have just thrown off is not my duvet. The rug I have just stepped on to is not my rug. These are not my pink painted walls, and those are not my curtains. I don't own that chair or that desk or that fuchsia, fleecy dressing gown, and I wouldn't be seen dead in those horrible slippers, which look like giant, hairy cat's paws.

I'm beginning to feel panicked now, even frightened. I don't understand why I'm wearing pyjamas, when I always sleep in a T-shirt. I can't work out how – overnight – my hair has seemingly grown long enough to tie into a ponytail, but when I brush the back of my neck with my fingers I am touching the knot of an elastic band. The long, thick strands it holds don't feel like they belong to me, and yet when I tug on them it hurts.

Everything is distorted, not quite real, like in the painting of a melting clock that I once saw in a book. This is my room, and at the same time, this is not my room. This is my body and not my body. I don't know where I am. I don't feel like myself. I know I should turn on the light and open the curtains, but I'm too scared. I don't want to walk past that mirror in case I see someone else looking back at me.

Some people have dreams so vivid that they think they're awake. Lucid dreams, I think they're called. That must be it: I must still be asleep, sleepwalking, the radio bleeding into my dreams. This is just a nightmare. It is not real. It will pass.

Maybe if I get back into bed and close my eyes and try to relax, I will wake up in a few minutes and everything will be normal again.

2

Reawakening

'Ella . . .'

My name. The sound of my mother's voice. I stir.

'Ella!'

I don't know how long I've been asleep for but it must have worked: I must be back in the real world, my nightmare over. When I choose to open my eyes, everything will be as it was yesterday. My mother is standing behind my bedroom door, her nagging tone the same as ever. God, I have never felt so pleased to hear it.

And now she is beating on the door. 'Get up! You're going to be really late. Ella!'

I moan. I am woozy, my limbs still too weighed down with fog to move. I can't hear the radio, so I must have slept through its hour-long cycle, or maybe it didn't come on at all. Perhaps I dreamed that too. The news is almost the same every day, with wars and bombs and politicians bleating on, and they always play the same music. It wouldn't be hard to invent a whole show. 'OK, OK, give me five minutes.' I yawn and stretch, pointing my toes towards the end of the bed, flexing my arms upwards and then out to the sides. I like the sensation, the sound of my joints clicking as they lengthen and snap back into place. It feels good.

And then my right arm catches something hard. A wall. The wall that shouldn't be there.

My eyes jerk open, even though I don't want to look. This is not happening, I tell myself. This is not possible. This is not true. But my eyes, my hands, my senses tell me different: I am still in the room that isn't quite right and that isn't quite mine.

My back arches and my stomach spasms, acid rising into my throat. Instinctively, I roll on to my left side and retch, vomiting onto the rug beside my bed. The horrible pink rug is now splattered with splotches of white and orange. It must be twelve hours since I last ate – since I remember eating – and so most of it is water. But it stinks. I lie still for a few minutes, watching as it dries into the rug, watching the fibres stick up and become matted. Then, because I don't know what else to do, I shout for help.

'Mum! Mummm!'

I'm seventeen, and taller than my mother, and we're not close, but at this moment I feel as helpless as a small child. She'll have an answer for me, an explanation. She'll make everything all right again, because that's what mums do. Even as I tell myself this, I'm not convinced. What possible reason could there be? Did mischievous elves break into my room while I was sleeping, redecorate and rearrange the furniture? Did those same elves put a magic potion in my food to make my hair grow several inches overnight, strip off my T-shirt and dress me in pyjamas, hide my phone and give me bad taste? I might even laugh at how absurd this sounds if I weren't so damn terrified. And if I didn't prefer it to the more likely explanation: that I am just going crazy.

'Muuuum!' I don't think she can hear me. Maybe she's gone downstairs to make breakfast, or she's in the shower, the gushing water filling up her ears. 'MUUUUUM!'

I feel too strange, too nauseous, too afraid to get up and find her myself. What if the rest of my house is different too? Perhaps there is no downstairs, no shower, nothing outside my bedroom door. Perhaps there is no house at all, just my room floating in space, my mother's disembodied voice an echo of another time. Perhaps I died in the night and this is some sort of afterlife, a punishment for all the bad things I did, the things I said. What did I do? What did I say . . . ? 'MUUUUUM! HELP ME!'

I hear footsteps. Lovely, familiar footsteps, evidence of a solid floor outside my room. She has heard me, she is coming now, and she will save me.

She bursts in through the door, without knocking, switching on the light before I can ask her not too. Too bright. Too pink. I shut my eyes instinctively.

'Ella, what's wrong?' I hear her say. 'What's happened? Why aren't you up? Are you ill?'

9

I nod and place my hand across my face. My eyes still screwed shut against the light, I bury my face under my duvet and point to my left side. 'I . . . I've been sick. I'm sorry.'

'Oh dear, love, and you didn't make it to the toilet.'

I nod again. How can I tell her that I was too scared to leave the room, unsure if there really was a toilet outside?

'Now you're not going to be sick again, are you? I can get you a bucket, if you need one.'

I shake my head. 'No, no, I don't think so.'

I hear her dragging the rug away and rolling it up, and then the bed bounces gently, as she sits down next to me. She takes my hand. I start to sob with the relief of not being alone.

'There, there,' she says. She must think I'm crying because I'm not well. Like a baby. I'll let her think that; anything is easier than trying to explain. 'It's OK, love.' The familiarity of her voice is soothing. She pulls me into her side and strokes my back. Even through the thickness of the duvet she feels like my mum, warm and soft, a small roll of fat poking above the top of her waistband. 'Don't worry, there's no harm done. I can put your rug in the machine. It'll come up good as new.'

A little calmer now, I laugh through my tears. It seems that, whatever I do to it, I'm stuck with the hideous rug. And then more tears come as it strikes me that Mum doesn't think – vomit aside – that there's anything different or strange about the rug. She thinks it's mine. She hasn't expressed any surprise at all at the transformation of my room. Or, indeed, at my own transformation. She is stroking my curiously long hair now, as if she's done it a thousand times before. The panic starts to rise in me again, my heart pounding too fast.

'If you're feeling better, I think you should get out from under that duvet and try to sit up.'

'OK,' I say, even though it's the last thing I want to do. I'm not going to be sick again, but I don't feel the least bit better. I take several deep breaths.

'We should make sure you're not dizzy. You don't have a headache, do you?'

'No. I just feel a bit . . . weird.'

'Probably just a tummy bug. Come on then.' She stands beside the bed and passes her arms around my back. 'Sit up slowly and open your eyes.'

I do as she says, emerging from under the duvet, but keeping my eyes tightly closed, until I am sitting up against the headboard. Then slowly I open them, first the left and then the right. I turn to look at her, expecting to see her smiling at me, to feel reassured. Instead, what I see makes me want to throw up again.

Mum's chestnut-brown hair has turned almost completely *white*.

'Oh my God, Mum!' The words come out before I can stop them. 'What's the hell's happened to your hair?'

She jumps back and touches her hands to her scalp, as if to check that her hair is still there. Reassured that it is, she pats it down. 'What do you mean?'

'The colour . . . I don't understand . . .'

She laughs nervously. 'Yes . . . and?'

I don't know what to say. She won't have missed the expression of panic on my face; I can't conceal it. Now she looks scared too. 'I don't know . . . I mean, it's, er, a bit different. I think . . .'

But I don't think anything, at least nothing I can say aloud. I think I'm frightened. I think that perhaps this isn't my real mother. She sounds like my mother and – apart from the hair – she looks like my mother, but she can't be my mother. And it isn't as though she is any older. Her face is still the same. She must be a poorly finished replicant, on whatever planet this is that I've found myself.

'You know it's been going grey for a long time,' she says, looking at me as if I'm the alien. 'You're the one who told me it suited me better natural.'

I can't recall ever saying that. No. I *know* I didn't say that. She is lying. Her hair was brown yesterday. I'm almost positive I helped her wash the dye out myself, just last week, because her roots were starting to show.

'Did I? Oh. I guess I, er, forgot . . .' I begin, and then a giggle bursts out of me. I try to restrain it but soon I am laughing and laughing uncontrollably, until I'm shaking and gasping for breath.

'What's so funny, Ella?' Mum says impatiently. She looks as if she can't decide whether to be annoyed or concerned.

I try to stifle my giggles by clearing my throat and just about manage to say, 'Don't worry about it.' Nothing is funny. It's so completely unfunny it's hilarious. I should probably pretend the hair thing was a bad joke or make up some story, but I don't have the energy.

We share an uncomfortable silence. I want her to leave now, my not quite right mother, but I can't think of a way to say it. I need some time alone to make sense of what's going on. I want to explore this bedroom properly, to try to locate my phone, to see if I can find anything I recognise. And I still haven't looked at myself in the mirror. I need to know that, long hair aside, I look like me.

'I think I should clean my teeth and have a shower,' I say eventually.

'Yes, of course. As long as you're not dizzy.'

Why does she keep asking if I'm dizzy? 'No, I'm not. I'm OK. My mouth just tastes gross and I need a wash.'

'Fine,' she says. She doesn't seem convinced. 'I'll come back and check on you in a while. I'll ring college and tell them you won't be in this morning. Call me if you need me.'

'OK.'

She leaves me alone, taking the rug with her. I wait for a minute, until I am certain she won't come back, and then I cautiously get up from the bed. Ignoring the horrendous cat slippers, I walk in my bare feet to the door, to make sure it is properly closed behind her. I notice it has a lock, which is peculiar, because I know Mum removed my bedroom door lock when I was about twelve. We argued about it when I said it meant she didn't trust me, and she said it was for my own safety. She'd read about some young girl with a locked door who'd died in a fire. She won, as always.

I steel myself to go over to the dressing table so that I can look in the mirror and face whoever it might be looking back at me. Casting my eyes downwards, I study the parts of my body I can see without its help: the shape of my pyjama-clad body, my hands and my feet. They seem normal enough. I will look more closely later, when I have a shower. It's reassuring to see that I am neither suddenly fat, nor too thin, that my breasts seem to be the same size, and that I haven't grown an extra thumb or lost a toe. I still have stupidly large feet. My toenails could do with a trim, and my fingernails show worn-off traces of a pink polish I don't use, but everything else is as it should be. This body looks and feels like it belongs to me, and it does as I command, moving and walking when I want it to.

And now my face . . . I take a deep breath and peer into the glass. Two tired-looking grey eyes stare back at me, wide with anxiety. They rest above a nose that is slightly too long, round cheeks and a mouth with a well-defined Cupid's bow. These are the features I know: my features. They are still arranged in the correct order and they don't look any older. I exhale with relief. While it may not be the prettiest face, at least it is my face. What's disconcerting, however, are the details that aren't quite right. My eyebrows are too bushy and look like they've never been plucked. The mousy-coloured hair, which frames my face, is too light and about four inches too long, with no fringe. There is also a faint red scar on my forehead, just above my right eyebrow. It appears quite fresh, as if there was a cut that is still healing. I don't know how I got it. But then nothing I have seen so far today makes sense. The only thing that hasn't changed at all is the sound of the voice in my head. The more confused I feel, the louder and more panicked it grows. It's starting to give me a headache.

With the light on I can now confirm that this bedroom is an almost entirely foreign place. It appears to belong to someone younger than me, someone I probably wouldn't choose to be friends with, someone who not only likes to paint everything pink, but who also puts up posters of cute cats cuddling and signs that say, 'Keep Calm and Carry on Dreaming'. If the misplaced furniture were not disorienting enough, a shelf seems to have levitated on to the wall above the bed. On it is a clock radio – one that does actually look a lot like mine (a present from my parents for my eleventh birthday) – but it is tuned to a commercial station I never listen to. Curiously, my old cuddly dog, Patch, who I couldn't bear to throw out but had hidden away in a cupboard, is leaning against it. There is also a pile of books, none of which I've ever read or even heard of, and, at the top of the pile, I spy a mobile phone. It is not my missing phone. Mine is shorter and wider and has a hard, shiny black shell. This one is in a battered, cream plastic cover, decorated with red hearts. For a split second, I wonder if it's wrong to pick it up and look at it, in case I'm invading someone's privacy, and then I realise how ridiculous that idea is. If this phone isn't mine, then who else might it belong to, and how did it get here? And even if it is someone else's, it's the only thing I have right now that might help to explain what's happening to me.

The phone is, frustratingly, switched off and it seems to take forever to come back on. When finally it does, it greets me with an irritating command:

Enter your passcode

Great. What the hell is the passcode? For want of a better idea, I try mine. It doesn't work, of course. So I input every combination of numbers that come to mind: my 'lucky' numbers, the last four digits of my best friend Deeta's phone number, even my own birth date. The phone doesn't accept any of them, continuing to blink four empty boxes at me. Exasperated, I try *1, 2, 3, 4* because I've read that it's the most common PIN, although, if this phone is supposed to belong to me, I can't imagine I'd be stupid enough to use that for security. To my surprise, and slight disgust, it works. I'm in. My first thought is to text someone to ask if they know what's going on. But what could I write?

Hi, it's Ella. I woke up this morning and everything is weird. My bedroom has turned pink, my mum's hair has gone white and I don't look quite the same. And I'm not sure even sure if this is my phone. Help!

They'd have me sectioned.

This phone is a different make from mine, so it takes me a while to figure out how to use the menu, and how to decipher the icons. Eventually, I find the address book and begin to scroll through it, starting with the favourites. Part of me is hoping against hope that none of the numbers inside are mine, so that I can confirm this isn't my phone, and that therefore this isn't my room, and there must be some sort of logical explanation for the rest. But, much as I wish that it wasn't true, I'm beginning to accept that the problem almost certainly doesn't lie with the room, or its contents, or with my mother, but with me. I'm the thing that is misplaced, distorted, lost.

The address book is a jumble of my contacts and someone else's. Mum's number is in there and so is my gran's, and a few friends who I've known since I started school, although we're not close any more. Who, though, are Rachel and Jen, and why do I have their numbers, not only in 'my' phone, but in my favourites list too? Why isn't Deeta's number there? I check several times but it has vanished; where it should be there are just entries for 'Dentist' and 'Doctor'. Anxiety rises up in me. Billy isn't there either, not a trace of him. I know that he hurt me and that I was planning to finish with him again, but I'm certain I didn't delete his number from my phone last night. I'd remember if I had.

There are no photos of him. Or of Deeta. There aren't many photos of anybody on this phone, just a few slightly blurry images of girls I don't know, their arms around each other, pouting at the camera. If there are other images, they must be stored elsewhere. Is there a laptop or tablet somewhere in this room? I will have to take a look later.

Perhaps reading the texts on this phone will make things clearer. I'm about to start scrolling through them, when I hear Mum calling from downstairs. 'Ella! Are you getting in the shower? Are you OK now?'

'Yes, yes. I'm just about to, Mum!'

I don't want her to come upstairs again. The texts will have to wait.

Before I pluck up the courage to venture outside and see what the rest of this house looks like, I have the urge to do something, although I'm not sure why. I lift the phone, hold my arm out as far as I can stretch it and take a photo of myself. I don't pose, or smile, I just look straight into the camera and press the button. Click. The girl in the picture gazes back at me, daring me to deny that she is me. I can't.

Somehow, viewing this new version of myself in a photograph cements my appearance, in a way that looking at my mirror image did not. I've never given it much thought before, but when you see yourself in the mirror – even when the world isn't strange and you know that you look like you – you're not seeing the 'real' you because everything, from the slight asymmetry of your features to your blemishes to your parting, is reversed. When you look at your image in a photo, you are seeing yourself as other people see you. And, at this moment, I am someone else too, a stranger to myself.

3

When I Was Me

Yesterday, when I was me, I had a life. It wasn't a particularly great life, but it wasn't a terrible one either, and at least it was mine.

This is who I was.

My name was Ella Samson and I was seventeen years and three months old. A Gemini, if that matters to anyone. I lived with my mum in a small North London house, the house where I grew up, and I saw my dad at weekends. Most weekends, anyway. Fewer since he married my new stepmum, and seeing him meant spending time with her. She didn't much like me, and the feeling was mutual, but that was OK because at least Dad was happy. Mum was happier too, in the end, after the divorce. And me? It's hard to say. At least there were no more dinner-table silences or painful arguments that leaked through my bedroom wall.

There was nothing extraordinary about me. I was an only child, but I didn't generally feel lonely. I went to a large sixth-form college, just up the road, together with most of the people I knew from school. I suppose I was hoping to go to university at the end, although I didn't study as much as I should have, and I'd mucked up my GCSEs, which meant I had to change my A-level options and give up on my dream of becoming an architect. I had a best friend called Deeta and an on/off boyfriend called Billy. There were other friends too, a group of them; we spent our evenings hanging around, watching films, listening to music, occasionally getting stoned. Normal things. Sometimes I felt bored, although I never said it.

There isn't much else to tell. I liked music, I was good at art, I read graphic novels. And I probably spent too much time online. I did some stupid things, and some things I wasn't proud of, things I wish I hadn't done and could take back. But doesn't everyone?

Yesterday, when I was me, I woke up in a room with cream walls and a beige carpet. I didn't own anything pink, and hadn't done since I was about thirteen. In fact, people often mistook me for a Goth or an emo because I liked to wear black and I dyed my hair darkest brown. I'd had it cut into a bob with a thick straight fringe, like the silent movie star Louise Brooks. There was a poster of her on my bedroom wall. I thought she was beautiful and mysterious. Deeta liked old, silent movies too. She was the one who introduced me to them, way back, after we first met at a friend's birthday party, and we bonded by watching them together. We had an intense relationship, the type where you tell each other absolutely everything and are so close that, sometimes, you're not sure where your personality ends and hers begins.

Yesterday, when I was me, I remember waking up late, tired from the night before because I'd been to a party. I hadn't enjoyed it much, because I'd argued with Billy, and he'd sloped off somewhere with his friends. That wasn't anything unusual; it was just happening more often lately. I remember doing some college work, taking twice as long over it as I should have because Deeta kept messaging me, and there were too many funny videos on YouTube, and because I wasn't all that interested in the essay I was supposed to be writing. Then I had Sunday lunch with Mum, faffed about with my essay a little more, and went to meet Deeta for a coffee. We ended up staying out into the evening, getting chips from the chicken place on the way home. It was an average day, a normal day. There were no signs that anything weird was about to happen.

And last night, when I was still me, I'm sure I went to bed in a room with cream walls and a beige carpet. I'm certain I checked my black phone three times before I went to sleep, to see if Billy had texted me back. He hadn't. I think I went to sleep wondering how he would act when I saw him at college, regretting not finishing that essay, wishing the weekend wasn't over.

But that was yesterday, when I was me, fully me. Today, everything is different. And now I'm wondering if yesterday actually happened, if yesterday really was yesterday, or if yesterday and all the yesterdays that came before it were a dream. Memories are fallible, aren't they? It's what you can sense around you that is supposed to be true: what you can see, hear, touch, smell and taste. That's the first rule of science. So if my memories seem more real, more tangible, than the world I find myself in, what does that mean?

Either I have lost my memory.

Or I have lost my mind.

And if I am not me, fully me, then who am I?

4

Alarming Discoveries

I let the water wash over me until my eyes are sore and my skin is red and blotchy. It's comforting to feel the shower's hot jets hit my skin and run down my arms and legs; it helps me to feel more connected to this body. This body, which, now that I am naked, also reveals aspects that aren't quite right. There are several large, splotchy, yellowish bruises on my chest and shoulder, which indicate that at some point during the past few weeks I've bashed into something very hard, or someone has punched me. But I can't remember either of those things happening . . . and I would, wouldn't I? And, sorry if this is too much information, but I'm surprised to find that I haven't shaved down there, like I normally do. Billy didn't like it if I didn't, so I just went along with it. It's weird to see myself looking natural. Not as itchy, either.

I usually do my best thinking in the shower, and I have never needed to think more than I do today. The problem is that thinking isn't getting me anywhere, just round and round in circles. Instead, I try to practise yoga breathing, like Deeta taught me to do. Be strong, Ella, I tell myself as I inhale. Be calm, I chant, as I breathe out. Don't tell anyone how strange you're feeling because you'll make them nervous or suspicious. And, most of all, keep remembering who you were.

The bathroom looks pretty much the same, except I'm not sure which toothbrush is mine, so I take an unopened one from the cabinet under the sink. I watch the girl cleaning her teeth in the bathroom mirror and even though I can feel the brush on my gums and taste the coolness of the mint, it's a bit like watching someone in a film. Maybe that's how I should get through today: by acting. I'm good at acting – I played the lead in a school play once. The problem is, I'm not sure what my lines are.

Now for my costume. I walk slowly back to the bedroom, hoping against hope that it will have reverted to the place I remember. It hasn't. With a sigh, I open the wardrobe and rifle through the contents. These clothes are my size, but I can't imagine wearing many of them; they're too colourful, not my style at all. Eventually I find some black jeans, a faded grey vest, which I think is meant for sleeping in, and a black cardigan. I dress myself in them and stand in front of the mirror. I suppose, hair aside, that I look almost like myself. Make up will help. There's a cosmetics bag in the dressing-table drawer, with a few well-used items in it. I'm sure I have . . . had . . . a lot more make-up than this. Taking the stub of a black eyeliner, I smudge it around my eyes, the way I usually do, following it with a coat of mascara. Is it unhygienic to use someone else's eye make-up when that someone else is you? I guess that's not the sort of question you can find the answer to on Google. It strikes me that I couldn't be bothered to take off my make-up before I went to bed last night. But there was no trace of it on my face, or on the pillow, when I woke up.

'You look very drab,' Mum says, when I get downstairs. 'And it's such a sunny day.'

I shrug. 'Is it?'

She leans in to peer more closely at me. 'You do look tired. But I like the way you've done your eyes. Very striking. Did one of your friends teach you how to do that?'

Uncomfortable, I take a step backwards. 'Something like that.'

Breakfast doesn't appeal. I have a cup of tea and eat a slice of dry toast, while Mum hovers in the kitchen, watching me take every bite. It's all I can manage. Even though I cleaned my teeth for ages, there's still an acrid taste in my mouth.

'OK,' I say, when I've finished. 'So I'm going to go to college now.'

'I really don't think that's such a good idea, Ella. You still don't seem yourself. You're very quiet and withdrawn. Maybe you should give college a miss today. I can stay here with you.'

That, alone, would be all the proof I needed to know something very weird is going on. My real mother would never suggest I took the whole day off college, not unless I had a fever of a hundred and ten degrees. Does she want to

25

keep me here for some reason? Paranoid thoughts begin to rush through my head again. Is this some sort of experiment? Is she just pretending not to know there's anything abnormal about today? Get back into character, Ella. Don't let your mask slip.

'Don't you have to go to work?'

'Not really. There's not much on at the moment. I can do some work from home. I've already called them. It's fine.'

This doesn't sound like Mum, either. She was so keen to make a good impression in her new job, to prove how successful and independent she could be without Dad.

'If I stay here, I'll just mope around all day and get bored. Honestly, I feel OK now.'

'All right. But if you don't feel well again, call me. I'll be here.'

'Sure,' I say, forcing a smile. I get up from the breakfast table. 'Er, where's my bag?'

'It's in the hall, where you always leave it.'

She follows me out into the hall. There's a rucksack lying at the bottom of the stairs. This must be it. I hesitate for a second, before picking it up by one of the straps and swinging it over my shoulder. It's curiously heavy, but easier to manoeuvre than my usual black leather bag.

'OK, then. I'm off.'

I head for the front door, then hang back. Where am I going? I assume I still go to the same sixth-form college, but I can't think of a way of asking without worrying Mum. As far as I know, it's the only one nearby. I'll just have to turn up and hope for the best.

'Ella, wait! You should wear a jacket – in case it gets colder later. You weren't well and it is almost October now.'

I look, clueless, at the row of coats hanging from the rail by the front door. 'I'll be OK.'

'No arguments, Ella.' She picks up a green parka-style jacket and hands it to me. I tuck it under my arm. Then she leans over to kiss me on the cheek. I can't help recoiling.

Act, Ella, remember to act.

'I've just realised I've left my phone upstairs. I'd better get it,' I say, pushing past her and taking the stairs two at a time. When I get back downstairs, she's still standing there. I drop the phone into the front pocket of the rucksack and steer past her, touching her on the shoulder in a bid to seem affectionate. She looks hurt.

'Bye then.'

She gives me a sympathetic smile. 'Take care of yourself, Ella.'

'Yeah, you too.'

Outside on the street, I once again have the strange sensation that I have found myself on a film set. There's no doubt that this is my street, with its neat row of houses and garages set two by two on either side of a narrow road. But a set designer appears to have been at work overnight. Everything looks so much brighter and more colourful than I remember, or maybe that's just because I'm seeing it for what feels like the first time. In my head, my street is drab and grey, something that never moves or changes. It's like watching a black-and-white film suddenly transformed into Technicolor.

I walk to the end of the road and turn into the little crescent on the right. It's not where I need to go but I'm not quite ready to face college yet. Placing the rucksack on the wall outside a house, I unzip it and go through its contents. There's a set of house keys, with a pink heart keyring, a purse containing ten pounds and a few coins, and both a Zip card and a college ID card, with the same passport-sized photo of a grinning new me on them. My fake ID – the one that Billy got me, so I could go to a club with him – is, ironically, nowhere to be found. The rest of the rucksack is filled with textbooks, but not ones that I've read or even that match the subjects I'm studying. It's as if I have become brainier overnight and didn't muck up my exams after all, and am now doing A-levels in Maths and Chemistry. A sketchpad and some charcoals give me the hope that I am at least still doing Art, and there's a Thomas Hardy novel called *The Mayor of Casterbridge*, which suggests I am still taking English too, but my Film Studies textbook is missing. There is no laptop. No tablet. I curse myself for forgetting to look for them at home.

I take the phone out of the front pocket. The battery is low and I'm not convinced it will last the day. Its charger must be in the house somewhere – I'll have to look for that later too. Frustratingly, there aren't many texts; for some reason most of the old ones have been deleted. Perhaps someone doesn't want me to know too much. Or maybe this is a new phone, placed inside an old cover. Nothing from Deeta. Nothing from Billy. A few mundane ones from my mum: *What time will you be home?*; *Please can you pick up a pint of milk while you're out.* I scroll through them, trying to find something interesting, something useful. There's a long thread with someone called Jen, who calls me 'hon' and 'babes' and puts kisses and smiley faces at the end of all her texts. She keeps talking about a guy called Dom, someone she likes. She wants to know what I think of him.

I wrack my brains. Do I know anyone called Jen? She was in my favourites list. Could she be one of the mysterious girls in the photos? There is a girl at my college with that name, and I think she might hang around with someone called Rachel, but I don't know them. We're on nodding terms, that's all. Why would this Jen be asking for my advice on her love life? I read the replies that have supposedly come from me, from this phone, and they're just as affectionate: *I'm not sure if that's a good idea, hon*; *I don't want you to get hurt*; *Let's chat about it when you come round, hon.* We appear to be close, even old friends. How can this be? The life that I can't remember living must stretch back for weeks, months, years . . .

I realise that I am shivering. Dropping the phone back into the rucksack, I unfold the coat Mum gave me and drape it across my shoulders. Looking for clues is only confusing me more. What I need to do is to talk to people: people I trust. Perhaps if I can find Deeta, or Billy, or just some of my other friends, everything will become clearer.

29

5

Lost

It's like my first day at college all over again. I don't know
where I'm supposed to be, what I'm supposed to be doing,
can't find my locker. But at least there were a group of us from
school that day, all in it together. Now I'm on my own, and
it's just another day in the middle of term for everyone else,
and I'm not even sure who I hang around with. The locker
I used to have, the one next to Deeta's – or what I think is
Deeta's – is no longer mine. I know this because the small
key on the keyring in my rucksack doesn't open it. Nothing
is going to be easy today, is it? Nothing is going to fit. Today
just doesn't work. I glance around furtively. It's the middle
of a lesson period, so nobody is around. I should have at
least ten minutes to try every lock until my key works in one
of them. I feel jittery, like a thief, and I guess I am in a way;
I'm stealing someone else's identity because I no longer have
one of my own.

On my fifteenth or sixteenth attempt I'm lucky. My key

slides into a lock and the latch turns over, letting me swing open the door. I peer inside the locker. There's a floral printed scarf hanging from the hook, some books and, thankfully, a timetable stuck to the inside of the door. It says I should be in a Chemistry class. I feel yet another pang of anxiety. There is no way in a billion years that I am going to walk into the middle of that class, in a subject I shouldn't be taking, and am clueless about. Absolutely no way. I will wait here, kill some time until the class is over and try to find someone I know over lunch. The timetable shows that this afternoon is taken up by double English. At least I'll know what language they're speaking, might be able to act my way through that. And maybe, hopefully, by tomorrow, when the timetable tells me the day starts with Maths, everything will have gone back to normal.

I take the scarf out of the locker and hold it up to my face. It's soft and smells of a flowery perfume, not one I use, but it's quite a pleasant scent. So this is what I – the me I can't remember – smell like. I sit down on a bench and wind the scarf between my fingers, trying to imagine that it belongs to me, wondering where I got it from, when I might have worn it. I toy with the idea of putting it on, but that doesn't feel right, so I stuff it in the rucksack and pull out the phone again. Jen and Rachel have both texted. *Are you in today? Are you OK? Text back, hon, we're worried.* I ignore the texts because they're not really for me, because I don't know what to say in response to them, and switch it back off.

There are footsteps behind me. Someone is coming. I look up to see a tall, slim girl in tracksuit bottoms, her dark hair in a long plait. I recognise her as someone Deeta vaguely knows; we might even have been at the same parties. She acknowledges me and nods, but doesn't smile.

I clear my throat. 'Hey, um, have you seen Deeta?'

'Nah, she's not in today. The whole of Film Studies has gone on a trip.'

I feel a pang of jealousy. By rights, I should be on that trip, but according to the timetable and the contents of the rucksack I'm not taking Film Studies. It was my favourite subject, the one I was doing best in.

'Oh right, of course. I forgot. Will she be back tomorrow?'

She shrugs. 'Guess so. I'm seeing her tomorrow evening. Want me to pass on a message?'

'It's OK. I can text her myself. I have her number.' That is not strictly true, but I know it by heart.

'Oh sorry, I didn't know you were friends.' She sounds sarcastic. 'I'm one of her best mates and I've never seen you hanging out with her.'

Seriously? How can this girl say that she's one of Deeta's best friends? Can it be true that Deeta and I don't even hang out? It would explain why she isn't in my phone address book. I feel sick, like someone has died. Sick and irrationally angry. 'Yeah,' I say coldly. I hate that this girl thinks she knows Deeta better than I do. 'We are. Really good friends. I've known her for years.'

She stares at me. I can almost see her thinking, *Who is this freak?* 'All . . . right . . . then. I see. Well, hope you catch up with her.' She flashes me a nervous smile and turns away to get something out of her locker.

The lunchtime bell rings. I jump up, propelled by a sudden burst of energy that fuels my muscles and makes my heart pound wildly. All my anxiety and fear and confusion, the heavy, spacey feeling that I'm not quite here, not quite walking on solid ground, has been replaced by one overpowering emotion: rage. What is happening to me is not fair. It's cruel and unjust. I want my life back. I want my best friend back. I want answers.

My legs march me to the canteen. Food is the last thing on my mind, but it's somewhere to go, somewhere lots of other people will be. Out of all of those hundreds of students, there's bound to be someone I recognise and feel comfortable talking to, someone who recognises the real me, underneath this mask that I've been forced to wear. I loiter at the entrance, as a wave of students pushes past me to get ahead in the queue, looking left and right to see if I can spy a friendly face. The people I was closest to will all be on the Film Studies trip, but maybe there will be someone I know from English.

And then across the room I spot Billy, as he sits down at a table with a group of his mates. I forget that I'm supposed to be angry with him and feel a burst of happiness. He looks exactly the same as usual, with his messy dark hair that refuses to lie flat, and his crumpled T-shirt and jeans. It would be better if he were alone; I know some of the guys he's with and I don't feel comfortable around them. And, because of Billy's indiscretions, they almost certainly know a lot more about me – the real me – than they should. But Billy is rarely alone. This is probably the best chance I'll get.

I walk over to his table, and stand by his side, like an idiot, unsure of what to say. He has his back turned to me and doesn't notice me there.

One of his friends glances up at me and nudges him. 'I think she wants a word with you.'

Billy swings around but he doesn't get up. He looks me up and down and a smile forms on his lips. 'Hi. Do you want something?'

'I . . . We . . . You . . . It doesn't matter.'

He laughs, but not unkindly. 'Look, I'm just having some lunch and then I've got to be somewhere. What is it you're after?'

'I just wanted to talk to you . . . In private, preferably.'

'What about? You're in my year, aren't you? What's your name?'

I feel my legs buckle. 'My name? Seriously? Billy, it's me, Ella.'

'No one calls me Billy,' he says, irritated now. 'Except my mum. It's Will to my friends. What do you want?'

'Nothing,' I say. I can feel tears beginning to sting the backs of my eyes. 'I'll tell you another time. Sorry.'

I turn my back on Billy and his friends, ignoring the sounds of their laughter as I walk away. Tears are now streaming down my cheeks. I'm sure they'll be talking about the girl who marched up to him for no apparent reason and called him his mum's pet name for the rest of the afternoon. They'll probably rib him about it for days.

But that's not what hurts. God, I can deal with a bit of teasing. Easy. And I can tell when I've been played – and this wasn't it. One thing I know about Billy is that he's a rubbish actor, and a pretty terrible liar too. He was not mucking me around; I only wish he had been. Billy, or Will, or whatever his name is now, is very clearly not my boyfriend. He is not my ex-boyfriend either. In fact, I don't think he believes he's ever met me or spoken to me before. The devastating truth is he has absolutely no idea who I am. I think about the way he used to look at me, as if he wanted me and was proud of me and owned me, all mixed up together, and even though it sometimes made me feel uncomfortable, at least I knew I mattered to him. Now, I'm a nobody. Did I dream our whole relationship? Was it some sort of crush that got out of hand in my screwed-up head, a fantasy that I now believe was a reality?

People often say they feel gutted. I've said it myself, loads of times. But I don't think I really knew what it meant before. It feels like someone has taken a knife, cut open my stomach and removed all of my insides, piece by piece. I am empty.

Dazed, I walk along the corridor until I spot an empty classroom. It's one of the science labs. The door is unlocked, so I let myself in and sit down at one of the benches. I stare pointlessly at the whiteboard. It's covered in equations, meaningless equations, half rubbed away – just like my life, really. The tears keep coming, rolling down my nose and on to the bench in front of me, splashing off the Bunsen burner. I want to stop crying, but I can't. I'm shaking too, I realise, shivering and rocking backwards and forwards, until I don't have the energy to rock or cry any more.

Somebody has come into the room. I stiffen and turn to look, instinctively rubbing my cheeks in case my eyeliner has smudged and I've got panda eyes, although I feel so numb that I don't really care if anyone can tell I've been crying. It's a guy, too old to be a student, but young for a teacher. He's short and thin – wiry, I think you'd call it – and he looks like he's picked his clothes from a jumble sale box and then put them on in the dark. A crumpled yellow-beige shirt is tucked into his too-short jeans, which float above horrible brown sandals.

He stands by the door, holding it open. 'Excuse me, but I don't think you should be in here.'

I sniff and say, 'Oh, sorry,' and move as if to get up to leave. Am I supposed to know this guy? I watch him as he approaches, trying to work out if I've seen him before. He looks serious, intense. I hope I'm not in trouble for being here. That would really cap the day.

He shuts the door and comes closer. 'It's OK,' he says, waving me back down. 'You can stay where you are. Are you all right? You look upset.'

'Um, yes . . . No . . . Sort of.'

He smiles. 'Take your time. I'm Daniel.' He holds out his hand as if he wants me to shake it, so I do. Mine is wet with my tears.

I sniff again. 'I'm Ella.'

'Yes, I know. I've seen you around the labs. I think we might even have spoken once or twice.'

'God, really? I'm so sorry. That's so rude of me.' I glance at his features again. Maybe he doesn't look entirely like a

36

stranger. Have I met him? It's so hard to tell today. I should be polite. 'Actually, you do look kind of familiar.'

'Don't worry about it. I tend to stay in the background and keep out of the students' way. I'm the archetypal outsider. I prefer not to be noticed too much, to be honest.' He grins.

'Ah, OK, then. So are you, like, a teacher here?'

'Not exactly. I'm the lab technician. I'm here to help set up the chemistry lab, help with experiments, clean up, that sort of thing. General dogsbody for Mr Chambers, mainly.'

I'm clearly supposed to know who Mr Chambers is, so I can't show that I don't. 'Right.'

'I'm doing a PhD in Physics. Working here part-time helps me pay my way and gets me out the library.'

'A PhD?' He must be seriously brainy. 'Wow.'

He shrugs. 'Not such a big deal. So what about you, Ella? Is there anything I can help with? If you don't mind my saying, you do seem a bit lost.' He grins again. 'I can always spot someone who's having an existential crisis.'

'Yeah, I'm not having the best day. Everything's kind of . . . I'm just not feeling too well.' I can hardly tell him the truth, and anyway, I don't know where to start. I get up from the desk. 'No offence but I don't feel like talking right now. I think I'm going to go to the sick room and let someone know that I'm going to go home.'

'Probably a good idea,' he says. 'Look, I didn't mean to intrude. If you need to talk, anytime, you know where to find me. I'm actually a very good listener. Better not tell anyone that.'

'Thanks.'

I follow him to the door and he holds it open for me. 'Do you want someone to escort you to the sick room?'

'No, honestly, I'll be OK. It's fine. I'd rather be on my own.'

When I am halfway up the corridor, almost out of earshot, he says something strange. At least, I think he does. It's under his breath, so I can't quite make it out. It sounds like: 'Oh, but we are all on our own.'

I turn round. 'What was that?'

He smiles. 'Nothing. Just take care of yourself.'

And I realise that I was not supposed to have heard it.

6

Suspicious Minds

White-haired Mum greets me at the front door with an 'I told you so' expression on her face. She wanted to come to get me but I insisted on walking home alone. I said I needed the fresh air but, really, I didn't feel comfortable with the idea of getting in the car with her.

'I've made you an appointment for the doctor,' she says, before I've even taken off my coat or put down my bag. 'I spoke to your dad and we agreed it was best to get you checked out.'

Seriously? Mum and Dad don't speak unless they absolutely have to. Now she's using the word 'we' like they make decisions together, like they're a unit. Usually she calls him 'your father', and that's when she's being polite.

'You actually called Dad because I was sick? I bet he was pleased. Jeez, you're really overreacting.'

'Yes, hopefully we are, but it's only been a couple of weeks since your concussion, and they said we should keep an eye on you, so it's better to be safe than sorry.'

Concussion? What concussion? I desperately want to ask about it but I know that I can't because that will just worry her more. Concussion is what happens when you hit your head, isn't it? When you're knocked out? But I haven't hit my head, or at least I don't remember hitting my head. Instinctively, my fingers reach up to the scar on my forehead. As I stroke it, I recall the strange bruises on my torso and the fact that this morning Mum kept asking if I felt dizzy. I must have been in some sort of accident. I must have had concussion. That I don't have any recollection of it scares me, but, at the same time, it gives me a tiny speck of comfort. People get strange effects after concussions sometimes, don't they? They get confused. Maybe all of this weirdness can be explained away somehow.

'Fine,' I say. 'Take me to the doctor then, if you want.'

The surgery is, as it always has been, only a five-minute walk away. We go in a sort of crocodile, with me leading and Mum walking just behind, as if she's scared I might change my mind and dart off at any moment. We sit in the reception area together, silently, each picking up a magazine that we don't really want to read, and pretending to be absorbed by it. Mine is an old celebrity weekly, from months ago. It's full of boob jobs and break-ups and fat bikini shots. I try to recall if I recognise any of these stories, if I've read them before, but all the Botoxed celebrities look the same and so they all blur into one.

My name blares out over the intercom. '*Ella Samson go to room eleven. Ella Samson go to room eleven.*' I throw the magazine down and jump up. Mum gets up too. I'm old enough to see the doctor on my own, but she insists on coming in with me. I don't think she trusts me to tell the doctor everything. And, because I'm still not sure what sort of conspiracy she might or might not be involved in, the feeling is mutual.

'So, what brings you here, Ella?' The doctor studies me and I study him back, trying to remember if I've seen him before.

'I'm not really sure,' I say. If I were here alone, I might try to explain how weird I feel today, how detached, how almost nothing in the world makes sense. But I can't, not with my mum glued to my side like a prison guard. 'Mum said I should come. I was sick this morning. It's not a big –'

Mum butts in: 'It's not just the nausea, doctor. She's been saying some strange things, being a bit forgetful. She seems very withdrawn too, moody, not behaving like herself. And she got very upset at college and had to come home early.'

'I see. And how long has this been going on for?'

'Just today really,' Mum says. 'I think. But after her accident, well, we thought it was a good idea to bring her straight in to make sure she's OK. At the hospital they said to keep a close eye on her, to tell a doctor if anything seemed off.'

He nods. 'Yes, you were right to. You can never be too cautious with head injuries.'

Mum looks pleased with herself. The doctor is reading something on his computer screen. I try to peer over to see it, in case it reveals any information about me or my accident, but it's too far away and at the wrong angle.

'I'm going to examine you now, Ella. Is that OK?

'Yes, sure, I guess.'

41

He asks me to sit down on an examination couch, then shines a torch into each of my eyes, before taking a sort of hammer and hitting each of my knees with it. It tickles and makes my legs kick out, and I giggle. Apparently satisfied, he holds his hand up to my face. 'Right, I'm going to place my index finger in front of you. Now I want you to touch it and then touch the tip of your nose, as quickly as you can. Can you do that for me?'

'OK,' I say, puzzled. How is touching my nose going to show anything? But I do as he asks, touching his finger and then my nose, back and forth, until he says to stop. I feel like I'm acting again, except now I'm in an episode of *Casualty* or *Doctors*. Girl with Concussion, played by Ella Samson. Or, rather, Ella Samson, played by Ella Samson.

'Good. Now get up. Please walk from the bed to the door and back, heel to toe, like you would if you were walking along something very narrow.'

I do it, feeling ridiculous, conscious that both he and Mum are staring at me.

'Good. Now, come back and sit down. That all seems as it should be. Your balance and coordination are excellent. I'm going to ask you some questions. Some of them might seem a little strange.'

'OK.'

'Do you know what day it is, Ella?'

'Yes, it's Monday.'

'Good. And you know where you are?'

Does he think I'm an idiot? 'Of course. I'm in the doctor's surgery.'

'Right. And can you tell me what you did yesterday?'

The question catches me off guard. I remember yesterday perfectly, but I'm not sure if is the right yesterday – the one that matches with my mother's memory. So, if I wasn't with Deeta, as all the evidence suggests, then where was I? 'Um . . . er . . .' I need to be as vague as possible. Oh God, I'm taking too long to answer; I can tell by the doctor's expression. Take a guess, Ella. 'I, er, saw some friends.'

The doctor looks over at Mum.

'Yes, she met up with her two best friends, Rachel and Jennifer.'

Them again. No I most certainly did not.

'And where did you go?'

'Um . . . to their house. Er, to Jen's house?'

'I thought it was to Rachel's,' says Mum. She looks at me suspiciously, like she's caught me out in a lie.

'Yeah, we went to both.'

The doctor clears his throat. 'OK. You do seem a little hesitant, Ella. Perhaps it's just nerves. You must feel under pressure here. How about you tell me if you remember what happened in your accident?'

Oh God. Is it better to say 'no, nothing at all' or to make a stab in the dark and risk getting it completely wrong?

'I, erm, hit my head.'

'Indeed. But do you remember being in the car? Where you were going? Who you were with?'

I try not to show my shock. It was a car accident. How could I have forgotten a car accident? Are the bruises on my chest marks from a seat belt? I start to breathe too fast,

43

aware that I'm freaking out inside and mustn't show it. 'Not really. It's a bit of a blur? Is that bad?'

I hear Mum gasp.

'Don't panic, Mrs Samson. It could just be the trauma. Ella, I need to ask you this: could you have taken something that's affecting your memory? Drugs, perhaps?'

Could I? As far as I recall, I went to a party on Saturday night. All I drank was Diet Coke. Might someone have slipped something in my drink? You read about it all the time: date rape drugs that make people black out and have no idea what's happening to them. Drugs that cause horrible flashbacks and paranoia. Perhaps I'm on a crazy trip, hallucinating everything I've seen today, or else hallucinating a whole life before it. But I can't suggest that, not now, not without telling the doctor and my parents the truth about how I feel. And something tells me that isn't the explanation. I was fine all day Sunday. Could a drug take that long to kick in? Denial is the safest option: 'I don't do drugs.'

The doctor looks directly at me. 'Be honest with me, Ella. This is important. You won't get into trouble.'

'OK, look, I might have smoked a bit of weed, once or twice, but that's it. Hardly ever. Not recently. And nothing stronger.'

Mum looks horrified. 'Oh, Ella! When did you do that?'

I sigh. 'With some friends. It's not a big deal.'

'Which friends?'

What can I tell her? With friends she'll never have heard of because they no longer seem to be my friends? With friends who'd probably deny knowing me, if they were asked? With a boyfriend who doesn't know I exist?

'Just friends.' I pause. 'Rachel and Jen, if you must know. Look, I'm not a junkie. I've tried it a couple of times, that's all. Like everyone.'

Mum looks shocked. Poor Rachel and Jen. I have no idea why I said that. To seem more convincing, I suppose. I don't even know them and now my mother believes they're junkies or dealers.

The doctor sighs. I think, like me, he's wishing that my mum wasn't in the room. 'OK, I need to ask you some other questions now, Ella. Can you tell me, have you been hearing voices?'

'Voices? What do you mean?'

'In your head.'

'Only my own voice. Thinking, you know. Like everybody does.' It strikes me that I don't know for certain that everyone does hear a voice in their head when they think. It's not something I've ever asked anyone else. I've just assumed. Do they?

'And is this voice saying anything unusual, or telling you to do anything you don't want to do?'

'Like what?'

'Telling you to do strange things, or telling you to hurt yourself or anyone else?'

'No way!'

'OK, good. You understand I have to ask these things.'

I nod. This whole situation is bizarre, not to mention ironic. Here I am trying to convince the doctor I'm sane, when I'm fairly certain I can't be.

The doctor turns to Mum. 'I'm not sure what's going on here. It's probably nothing – just normal teenage stuff, possibly a post-traumatic reaction to the accident. The nausea may well be coincidental. But I think I'm going to refer Ella to the hospital for a CT scan, just in case. OK?'

'Of course,' says Mum.

He types something on his computer and then prints it out, handing it to her. 'Take this down to A&E and they should see Ella this afternoon.'

'Hold on,' I say. I don't know what a CT scan is, but it sounds serious. 'Why do I need a scan?'

'Just to have a little look at your brain to make sure everything appears normal.'

'My brain? And what will it show?'

'Hopefully, nothing.'

But it might show something. I might have brain damage, from an accident I don't recall. Perhaps there is something really terrible wrong with me, like a brain tumour, eating away at my memory bit by bit. Or maybe a scan will reveal that there's an object implanted inside my head – an alien chip or a transmitter.

And if it reveals nothing, then what?

I'm not sure if I'm more scared of finding out what's wrong with me than I am of not knowing.

7

My Beautiful Brain

I am lying completely still inside what looks like a white ring doughnut, my head held rigid within a soft brace, as invisible rays sweep over me and penetrate deep into my brain. I can't feel anything, can't see anything except the cold plastic of the tube surrounding me, can hear nothing but the gentle clicks and whirs of the scanner. It isn't dark and I know that I'm not alone – the radiographer is just a few metres away behind a window – but it feels like I am in a tomb. Trapped. Unable to move or escape. Trying not to panic, I close my eyes and force myself to imagine instead what the radiologist can see on her screen, as the scanner explores every hidden corner of my brain, up and down, left and right, deeper and deeper, as though it is peeling away the layers of an onion.

Click. What is hidden in there, inside my skull, at the core of me?

Whir. What or who has done this to me?

Click. How can I find my way back?

I wonder if the radiographer can tell that I am thinking about her right now, whether her equipment allows her to read my emotions and my thoughts, to decipher them. Might she even be able to control them? Maybe the whole 'accident' story is just a convenient ploy, and the doctors are in on it too, and what this scan is really for is to reset my brain, to reprogram me, to make me forget my past life entirely. No, that's just a stupid conspiracy theory, like something from science fiction. Isn't it? Whatever the truth of it, I know it's important that I keep thinking about the me I was yesterday. I must try to cling on to her, must try to push her into a safe crevice of my mind that the scanner can't reach . . . somewhere even my own doubts can't disturb her.

Click.

Whir.

Concentrating hard, I picture myself as I was, laughing with Deeta at a DVD, holding hands with Billy, wearing my own clothes, relaxing in my bedroom with my own things around me. But my mind keeps drifting, away from the past to the present: to the mother with white hair, to the Billy who doesn't know me, to the mirrors and shop windows that reflect back someone altered, someone changed. It drifts to the rows of college lockers that won't open for me, to the Bunsen burners in the science lab, to the walk home along my curiously Technicolor street. It drifts and drifts until I realise it's not just my mind that is drifting, but the whole of me. I no longer feel constrained by the scanner, but at one with it, breathing to its rhythm.

Click. Whir.

Click. Whir.

Now I am floating away from my body, gliding outwards and upwards to a place that is beyond the ceiling and its fluorescent lights, far above the scanning room, higher even than the roof of the hospital. I am weightless and free; not just in the air, but a part of it. When I look down I can see myself, motionless, my arms held tight to my sides, my head strapped down. I look so peaceful, so still, that I half wonder if I might actually be dead.

And then it hits me that the person I am looking down on in the scanner is not the girl who was brought to the hospital this afternoon. She has chin-length dark hair and a fringe. She is me: the old me. And I know with absolute certainty that this is not just some weird out-of-body experience; I am remembering something. Something that could be significant.

I have been in a scanner like this before. It isn't the first time, maybe not even the second. I can't remember being strapped down as I was today, can't recall changing into a hospital gown, or the radiographer's pep talk, or sliding inside the machine. But the clicks and the whirs, the bright lights, the hospital sounds and smells are, I now realise, all too familiar. Other ghost memories begin to flicker within me: an awareness of distant beeps, hushed voices, the sensation of a warm liquid burning through the veins in my arm. If only I could remember exactly what happened and, more importantly, why. I try to focus, to make myself grasp something tangible, but the harder I push, the less I can see. Where there should be facts and details, there is just a void . . .

'Ella . . . Ella . . .'

I slowly become aware that the clicks and the whirs have stopped. Instead, there is the crackle of the intercom, and a soft voice saying my name. I am no longer floating free. I am once again in the scanning room, trapped within the scanner. Worse, I am trapped back inside the new me.

Someone is gently touching my arm. 'I think you must have fallen asleep in there,' says the radiographer. 'We've finished. We're going to slide you out now. OK?'

I nod, but my tethered head doesn't move. Then I feel a pulling sensation, and I am gliding out of the doughnut. Above me the radiographer's smiling face slides into view, and then I stop moving and she leans across me to undo my head strap. 'Sit up slowly now,' she says, placing her hand on the small of my back to help me. I am woozy and a bit dizzy. I'm not sure if it's because of the rays that zapped through my brain or because of what I felt, what I think I remembered.

'Relax for a couple of minutes. I'll take you through to see the doctor with your mum, once you're dressed.'

'All right. Was everything OK, with my brain, I mean?'

She smiles. 'I shouldn't really say anything now, but it's good news. You can tell your mum that your brain looks absolutely perfect. You have a healthy brain.'

'Oh,' I say, trying to look happy. I'm pleased I don't have brain damage, obviously, but I was hoping the scan would show *something*. 'Can I just ask, how does it compare to the other scan I had? Was there anything weird on that? Anything different?'

'I'm afraid you'll have to ask the doctor about that,' she says.

There's a wait to see the brain doctor, so Mum and I sit in the waiting room together on hard plastic chairs and sip tepid water in polystyrene cups. She seems a little more relaxed, now that she knows there isn't a blood clot about to explode in my head, and that I won't suddenly drop dead or become a vegetable. I try to relax too, to be a little bit more friendly towards her. If I'm going to find out what's happened to me, I suppose I need to trust her.

We make small talk for a while, and then I pluck up the courage to ask her: 'So what exactly happened in my accident?'

She sighs. 'You really don't recall anything?'

'No, that's why I'm asking. It's a total blank.'

'It was a Saturday afternoon, a few weeks ago. I wasn't there so I only know what I've been told. Your dad was with you in the car, giving you a driving lesson. You were just a few minutes from home, on the main road near the bus stop. Apparently an old lady stepped out into the road, and you swerved to avoid her. You went into another car and hit your head on the steering wheel. You were out cold for a few seconds.' She pauses and her voice drops. 'For a moment, your dad thought you were dead.'

'Oh.'

I'm not sure what to say, or how to feel. It's like I'm hearing a news report about someone else. It's not just that I don't remember the accident; I don't even remember taking driving lessons, and can't imagine myself behind the wheel of a car. I know I wanted to learn to drive, the day I turned

51

seventeen. But both Mum and Dad made it very clear that I was 'in no way responsible enough, and it's too expensive'. When and why did they change their minds?

'Was the old lady OK?'

'Yes, she was fine, I believe. She disappeared off afterwards, completely vanished. No one could find her, which was a pain for the insurance.'

'What about the car I went into? The other driver?'

'They were fine too. Your dad's car took the brunt of it – it was a complete write-off – that's why he got the new one. Thank God you were wearing your seat belt. It's all your dad's fault. I told him he shouldn't give you lessons himself. You should have had a proper instructor, with a dual-control car, but he didn't want to pay for it.' She shakes her head. 'It's typical of your dad. He always thinks he knows best.'

I smile to myself. Mum slagging off Dad – that, I recognise. Some things don't change.

'Ella, are you sure you really don't remember any of it? Not even a bit?'

'Nothing,' I say, now on the verge of tears with frustration because I don't, can't remember. 'I said so, didn't I?'

She sighs once more, as though she is in pain. 'But if your brain scan is clear, then why on earth not? Oh, Ella. I don't like this. I don't like it at all.'

I shrug. I don't like it one little bit, either. And she still doesn't know the half of it.

I don't have to say anything more because the brain doctor calls us in. She has my scans in her hands, and a set of my notes. Like the radiographer, she seems delighted that my brain is 'perfect'. Some people have great legs, others great hair. Apparently, I have a beautiful brain. It's just my luck that nobody else will ever be able to appreciate its gorgeousness unless I leave my body to science and it ends up in a jar on someone's desk.

'So, we can discharge you back to your GP,' she says, clearly keen to get me out of her office as quickly as possible.

'Great,' I say. 'But I need to know if the scan shows anything different. From last time, I mean.'

'Last time?'

'The scan, or scans, I had before. Maybe something's changed. I guess they must have been done after the accident. But, well, I can't remember . . .'

She flicks through my notes. 'Previous scan? There's nothing here to suggest you've ever had a scan before. Certainly not at this hospital.'

'Really? But while I was in the scanner I remembered! I'm a hundred per cent certain. Are you sure it just hasn't got lost, or something?'

'No, it says here that you didn't need a scan last time you came. They just observed you for a few hours, then sent you home.' She turns to Mum. 'Has she ever been to hospital before?'

'Only when she was born,' Mum says. 'And for an X-ray, when she sprained her ankle.'

The doctor shakes her head. 'Then you must be mistaken, Ella. We don't perform CT scans unless it's absolutely necessary.'

'Oh. But then why did it all feel so familiar, when I was having it? Lying there, the smells, the sounds, just being there . . . I felt it.'

'Probably déjà vu. Do you know what that is? Your brain was probably playing a trick on you. It felt like it had happened before, but it didn't.'

'I guess . . .'

I wonder, for a second, if all of my memories might be a type of déjà vu: the sensation that I've experienced something that hasn't really occurred. Maybe when I saw Billy, I felt like I knew him, even though I didn't. But that wouldn't explain why everything that is supposed to be real and right feels unreal and wrong, would it? Not unless there is also such a thing as déjà vu in reverse – when what you supposedly have experienced feels unfamiliar, and like a dream.

I can't be hiding my emotions too well because the doctor notices. 'I've never seen anyone look so disappointed about a clear scan,' she says, touching my arm. 'You're fine. You can go home now.'

'But if my brain's OK, then why don't I remember the accident?'

'I'm not sure. There's a lot we still don't know about the brain, and some people do have a few problems after a concussion. I'm not a psychologist but I suppose it's possible that the accident was such a big shock that you've blocked it out. A type of amnesia caused by psychological trauma. I'll write a letter to your GP to suggest you have some counselling.'

Psychological trauma? Is she saying I'm like the poor World War One soldiers I read about at school, who lost their minds because of shell shock? There hasn't been a war, just my stupid head making contact with a stupid steering wheel.

'Don't worry,' she says. 'Talking about it will help. And there's no reason why your amnesia should be permanent. Your memory will come back. You probably just need to take it easy for a little while, have a few days off college.'

'Sure,' I say, forcing a fake smile. 'I'll take some time out. I'll be fine.'

She starts speaking to Mum but I'm not really listening any more. I don't have faith in her, or in medicine, to explain what's happened to me. Whatever she says, this can't just be amnesia. Of that I am certain. Because I know what amnesia is: it's when you forget the things that have happened. Amnesia doesn't make you remember experiences – certainly not a whole chunk of your life – that haven't occurred.

8

Playing Happy Families

We arrive home from the hospital to find Dad waiting for us in the kitchen.

I don't understand what he's doing here, when he should be at work, or at his own house, and when Mum said very clearly that she wouldn't let him back through the front door over her dead body. I don't even know how he got inside the house because I watched him hand the keys back to her when he moved out. He used to have to wait in his car when he came to pick me up, so that Mum wouldn't have to see him – or his 'smug, duplicitous face' as she put it. He'd honk his horn a few times to let me know he'd arrived and I'd go out to greet him, while she sulked in the hall. And yet, now, here he is sitting at the kitchen table, with a cup of tea, and his laptop in front of him, as if he belongs here.

But he doesn't, not any more. Or, at least, he didn't.

'Ella, darling,' he says, getting up to hug me. 'I was so worried. Are you OK?'

I don't have brain damage, if that's what he means, but I am very much not OK. Seeing him has thrown me off kilter again, and to be honest, I'm not sure how many more jolts I can cope with today. I back away from him. 'What the hell are you doing here?'

Dad blanches. He looks like I've slapped him, and I feel bad because I didn't mean to say it aloud.

'Ella! Don't be so rude!' says Mum. I watch, incredulous, as she walks over to him and touches him on the shoulder, almost affectionately. 'He left work early because he was worried about you. I told you, I called him.'

'Sorry. I was just . . . surprised. That he's here in the house – and that you both seem happy about it.'

She furrows her brow at me. 'Are you being sarcastic?'

'No, not at all.

Mum looks at me as though I'm some sort of human conundrum. I sit down at the table and watch in silence, as she reassures Dad that I'm not myself today and fills him in on what happened at the hospital – how I probably have 'shell shock' and need therapy. I suppose I should be glad that they're being civil to each other, even if it must only be because they're both worried about me. But, like everything else that's happened today, it's unsettling.

Dad smiles at me, the way people smile at little old ladies and sick or disabled children. Sympathetic. Concerned. Patronising. I smile back blankly. I can't help noticing that he looks more stressed and older than I remember. His forehead is starting to resemble a piece of graph paper, the criss-cross lines much more deeply etched. And yet, as far

57

as I can pinpoint in my screwed-up, unreliable brain, it's only been a week since we saw each other. Unless he's had reverse Botox, how can that be?

'I'm going to make some dinner,' says Mum. 'Spaghetti all right? Do you think your stomach can handle it, Ella?'

'Sounds good,' says Dad, before I can respond. Mum disappears into the kitchen.

I look at him, wide-eyed. So now he's staying for dinner? This show of solidarity is going a bit too far. It's not as if I'm dying, not physically, anyway. 'Aren't you going to go home for dinner, Dad?' I say cautiously, so he doesn't think I'm being rude again. 'Won't Tamsyn be waiting for you?'

He laughs. 'Tamsyn?'

'Your wife. My stepmother. You know, the one who wears short skirts and high heels, and who's not that much older than me.'

'Very funny,' he says. 'My other family has gone on holiday, so I'm safe.' He winks, as if we're playing a game. 'Don't worry, you're still my favourite daughter.'

He pinches my cheek, and I realise that he's not joking around. He genuinely seems to have no idea who Tamsyn is. My stomach lurches. This is like my experience with Billy all over again.

I launch myself up from the table and, almost tripping over my own feet, rush into the hall. Right in front of me is all the evidence I didn't notice earlier, because I was too busy trying to find 'my' things: Dad's shoes are in the hall cupboard, his old cagoule on the coat rack, his umbrella in the stand. I take the stairs two at a time, arriving out of breath in the bathroom. Inside the cupboard above the sink is Dad's shaving brush, his shaving foam and razor. There are three, not two, toothbrushes in the toothbrush holder – four if you count the new one that I opened.

All of this can mean only one thing: Dad still lives here. He has never left.

And it means that I must have imagined, dreamed or conjured up the whole long, tortuous divorce, his affair, remarriage and the uncomfortable weekends with Tamsyn at his new house. My brain has somehow created its own version of a wicked stepmother fairy tale.

Just how screwed up am I?

I take a few minutes to calm myself down and then go back downstairs to face my parents. They're both sitting at the table, looking anxious, when I return.

'What's wrong?' says Mum. 'Dad said you just jumped up and disappeared upstairs. Were you sick again?'

I nod. 'I just felt nauseous, but I didn't actually throw up. Listen, I don't really think I'm up for a big meal tonight. Can I just have some toast and a banana or something, and take it up to bed? I need to rest.'

'Of course. You'll be much more comfortable in your bedroom. We'll come to check on you in an hour or so.'

'Thanks.'

As I trudge back upstairs, carrying my meagre dinner, it occurs to me that Mum is wrong; I don't actually have anywhere comfortable, or familiar, or safe to go. There is nothing in the world that belongs to me any more, not the room itself, or any of its contents. If there had been a fire, I could, at least, have saved a few possessions: some photos or old diaries, or cards. But I had no warning that I was about to lose everything.

I lie on the bed for a while, staring up at the ceiling, feeling sorry for myself. I sit up to eat the by now cold toast and half the banana, and then I curl myself into a ball, and will myself to go to sleep. But sleep doesn't come and, after a while, I grow bored of keeping my eyes shut and trying to quieten my racing brain, and decide to get up and do something. It would make sense to explore the room in more detail, but I realise quickly that I don't have the energy to go through cupboards or drawers, or even to read. Instead, I tune the radio in to the station I used to wake up to, and lie back on the bed to listen. They're playing a track I like, the one by the band that Deeta wanted to buy tickets to see next month. The Wonderfulls, they're called. I sing along in my head, pleased that I can still remember all the words. And it strikes me, yet again, how almost everything outside of my own life seems to be the same as it was. It's as if the world has been turning in one direction, while I've gone in another.

Someone is coming up the stairs. I turn down the radio and rearrange myself on the bed, so it looks like I've been sleeping. There's a cautious knock on my bedroom door.

'Ella, are you asleep?'

'Nah, Mum. I'm awake.'

'Can I come in?'

'Yes, OK.'

She enters the room and I notice that she has something in her hand. 'Your phone was ringing,' she says, holding the phone out towards me. 'It was downstairs, in your bag. It's Jennifer. I thought you'd like to talk to her.'

I make a face at her. If it were my own phone, in my own bag, I'd be angry with her for snooping. But I realise I don't care about that at all; I feel anxious, not annoyed. I am completely unprepared to talk to Jen – I've never spoken to her before, and yet I'm supposedly her best friend. What am I supposed to say? To sound like?

'OK, I'll take it,' I say, making an instant decision. It's not the easy option – I could just have said I didn't feel like talking, that I'd call her back. But I figure that if I keep ignoring Jen and Rachel, they might stop ringing and texting. And, at the moment – even though I don't know them – they're the only friends that I'm aware 'I' have. I take the call because I think – hope – that perhaps Jen can help me to figure out what's going on. Most of all, I take it because I'm feeling lonely, and I want to talk to someone.

I motion to Mum to leave the room and she nods at me, pausing to pick up my empty plate and scoop up some crumbs from the duvet cover before she goes. She leaves me the half-eaten banana. When I'm sure she's out of earshot, I take a deep breath, clear my throat and nervously hold the phone to my ear, like someone who has never used one before. 'Hello?'

'Hey,' says a warm, bright voice, 'I just wanted to make sure you were OK. You weren't in college today and you didn't text me or Rachel back. We were worried.'

'I'm sorry. I meant to.' I don't correct her about college. I'd rather that she doesn't know I was there and didn't come

61

to find her. 'I just haven't been feeling too well, and I've been to the hospital.'

'God, Elle,' says the voice, sounding genuinely concerned. 'What happened?'

'Nothing. Don't worry. I puked this morning and they thought I should have a scan. It's to do with my accident . . .' I leave it hanging there, unsure what Jen might know about the accident, hoping she might fill in the gaps.

'But that was weeks ago and you were OK. We saw you yesterday and you were completely fine. Weren't you?'

Was I? 'Well, I guess it's like a delayed reaction, or something.'

And so I tell her the official version: that I have post-traumatic amnesia. She swallows it, like it makes perfect sense, gasping and giving me words of sympathy and concern in all the right places. I think she sounds sweet, that she must be a kind friend. And, as we speak, I decide that this will be my story: I'm going to tell everyone that I have amnesia. It's easy, convenient, it makes sense. If I say something strange? Blame the amnesia. If I do something bizarre? That damned amnesia again. I'm going to let people think that I have lost my memory following an accident, even though I don't believe that is the truth. Far better to be known as a victim, as the girl who can't remember, than as the weird girl, the freak, the misfit. I'd rather people felt sorry for me than avoided me.

'So when are you coming back to college?'

'I don't know. They said I should rest, have some time off. In a couple of days, maybe.'

62

'Of course. Listen, don't worry about your work. Rachel and I will take notes for you and fill you in. We won't let you get behind.'

'Thank you. That would be cool.' I smile to myself. If only she knew that I am already behind – several years behind, in fact, in subjects I've never studied.

'Don't mention it. So when can we come round to see you? We can bring grapes and puzzle magazines and a big box of pampering stuff.'

I laugh. I haven't liked puzzle magazines for years. And beauty treatments aren't my thing. 'I guess you can come tomorrow evening. You don't have to bring anything. I'll text you if I'm not up to it.'

'Perfect,' she says. 'I'll leave you to rest now. See you tomorrow, hon.'

'OK, Jen.' I can't bring myself to be more familiar. Even saying 'Jen' seems weird. 'See you tomorrow.'

I end the call and breathe out loudly. That went OK, I think. And now I've got about twenty-four hours to prepare myself to meet her and Rachel, to find some more evidence of our friendship, to check out their online profiles and study their photographs. Tomorrow I am going to spend the day exploring my room and the house, to find things that will give me clues as to who I am supposed to be . . . But maybe I won't have to. Maybe, just maybe, when I wake up tomorrow, everything will have gone back to normal. If only that could happen. If only I could have my life back and be me again. I suppose that if I believed in God I would say a prayer right now, but I don't. I've always thought that it seemed wrong to pray on the off chance that someone, or something, might be listening. Imagine if they answered, and your prayer was realised. Where would that leave you?

Tiredness is beginning to overtake me at last. I yawn and stretch, acknowledging that every part of me aches. It's only just after nine but I think I should get ready for bed, try to sleep, put an end to this hideous, topsy-turvy day. Rejecting the pyjamas that I found myself wearing this morning, I go to the wardrobe and root around until I find an old T-shirt that I can sleep in. It's a little too short to be decent, barely covering my bottom, but nobody will see me in it, and so who cares? Then I switch out the lights and climb into bed, covering myself with the duvet. I can't be bothered to clean my teeth, or to wash my face. That doesn't matter, not today. Perhaps, I tell myself, if I lie completely still, in the darkness, with my eyes shut, I can somehow transport myself into my old body, into my old room. I can at least try to imagine that today didn't happen.

I don't know how long I've been in bed, or what time it is, or whether I've managed to sleep at all, but at some point I become aware of raised voices from the room next door. I strain my ears, to try to make out what they're saying, but I can only decipher a few words: 'Stupid!'; 'Impossible!'; 'Idiot!'; 'Bastard!' My parents are playing squash with insults again, hitting them back and forth against my bedroom wall. I sit up, confused, alarmed. Dad shouldn't be in Mum's bedroom. He slept in the spare room for at least a year before he moved out; it must be three years since I've heard them at it through the wall. But even though it's horrible to hear them screaming at each other, there's something comfortingly familiar about it. It feels more real than their show of unity earlier.

I climb out of bed and tiptoe over to the wall, pressing my ear up against it. I need to know what this argument is about.

'Stop blaming me for your mistakes,' I hear Mum saying.

'Why? Because it's always my fault?' says Dad.

'It invariably is,' says Mum.

'Oh really? You're the one who shouldn't have let her go to college today. It's clear she wasn't up to it.'

'Yes, probably not, in retrospect, but she insisted she was OK. She's seventeen, not seven. And you weren't around, as usual, so I had to make the decision myself. Not to mention she wouldn't have got into this state if it weren't for you.'

'My God, that's low, even coming from you!'

'Maybe, but it's true. I said we should get her a proper driving instructor. But no! You wanted to save money and you just had to teach her yourself, even though you've got no experience and you had a completely unsuitable car. Didn't you?'

'And who was I trying to save money for? For you! For us!'

'At the cost of our daughter's health? That worked out well, didn't it?'

'It was an accident! It could have happened to anyone. The old woman ran out into the road! Do you know what? I've had enough of this. I can't be around you.'

The voices stop. Then I hear a slammed door, thudding footsteps on the stairs, the sound of the front door opening.

Dad has stormed out of the house, just like he always used to do. He'll be sitting raging in the car now, driving round the block until he calms down. In an hour or so, he'll come back and there will be a sort of truce, until the next time.

I retreat back to bed, folding my knees into my chest, trying not to cry. Despite everything else that has changed, my parents still hate each other and they are still arguing about me. They really shouldn't be together. So why are they? How are they?

I used to blame myself for the divorce. I used to think that if I'd behaved better, done my homework on time, come back when I said I would, not got into trouble with boys . . . that my parents wouldn't fight. But as far as I can tell, I am no longer that person. And now it feels like it is my fault that they are still, unhappily, together.

9

One Hundred and Fifty-five Thousand People

The morning light glows sickly pink.

My fingers touch hard wall.

And for one horrible, heart-sink moment, I don't want to get out of bed. Ever again.

The prayers I didn't say haven't been answered. It has now been a whole twenty-four hours since everything changed, the world has made a full revolution around its own axis, and here I am, still trapped inside the girl I don't recognise. It feels as if the person I used to be is slipping further and further into the past, and I have a dread fear that she might not ever return.

I bury myself under the duvet and scream silently, fighting the urge to pound my head against the wall that shouldn't be there. To pound and pound and pound until my face and my brain are obliterated, and I don't exist any more. My back and my feet and my jaw tense up, and I curl myself into a ball, like a cat that's about to attack, clenching my fists so hard that my fingernails bite into my palms. When it starts to hurt too much, when I can't hold that position any longer, I let go. The tension spills out of me, muscle by muscle, sinew by sinew, until I am just a floppy bag of bones and skin sinking into the mattress. I feel calm now, almost relaxed. There's no more fight in me. And then I start to think. While what's happened to me is beyond weird, perhaps my experience is not altogether unique. Life can't be predicted. I once read that one hundred and fifty-five thousand people in the world die each day. How many of them know it will happen today, or expect it?

Today, somebody, somewhere, is climbing out of bed, with no idea that in two hours' time they will walk into the path of a speeding car, a car they won't see or hear. And they will never see or hear anything again. Yesterday, they might have booked tickets for a gig next month, or bought a dress they'll never wear. Yesterday, they believed they had a future. Tomorrow, they will exist only in the past.

Today, a confident woman will take a wrong turn and find herself face to face with a mugger, who will threaten her with a knife, take her handbag and leave her too scared to go out alone.

Today, a newsagent will step outside for a breath of fresh air and notice how his shop sign flaps in the wind. He will think about calling someone to repair it, moments before a gust of wind sends it crashing on to a passing customer's head.

Every day people wake up, unaware that before the sun goes down, their lives will change forever. And all these people went to bed last night expecting today to be like any other day. Like yesterday. What makes me so special? I might not be me, but at least I'm still here, still alive, unbroken.

I push off the duvet, so swiftly and with such force that, dragged over by its own weight, it falls to the floor. My body now exposed, I look down my legs, my feet, and I realise that it's not even as if it is the first time that I have changed. I didn't always have this body, with limbs this shape or length. Once I was a baby, tiny and helpless and unable to speak. I was hairless and chubby-cheeked, with fingernails the size of lentils. She was me, I can't deny that, and yet I look nothing like her, can't remember being her, have no idea what she thought or felt.

Once I was a small child, playing with dolls, afraid of witches and monsters. I wore my hair in bunches and refused to talk to boys. That little kid, with her high-pitched voice and scabby knees was me too, even though it's impossible to think myself into her mind or her body.

The truth is, I have already lived many lives in my lifetime; there have already existed more versions of me than I can count. I have been constantly changing, little by little, cell by cell, pore by pore. All these other transformations were so slow that I simply didn't notice them happening. This one is different only because it was so violent and sudden, because it happened overnight.

The more I think, the more hopeful I begin to feel. I might not know who I am right now, but I know who I was. Perhaps I can begin to claw myself back to her. Perhaps, bit by bit, I can become her again. And I can start today. I can start right now.

10

Reinventing Ella

I get up, shower and dress at breakneck speed. My energy feels limitless. There is so much to do, so much to discover, and I need to start immediately. Yesterday was a day for grieving, for being batted from one shock to the next, for flailing about helplessly and for wanting to run away. Today I am taking control.

Having eaten so little in the past twenty-four hours, I feel ravenously hungry, and so I wolf down a bowl of cereal and two rounds of toast with mashed banana, as Mum watches on in bemusement. 'You're like a different girl today,' she says, and I can't help smiling at her choice of words. 'I'm glad to see you're feeling better.' I nod and mumble something about being right that it was just a one-day bug, and absolutely nothing to do with my accident. For a moment I worry that my miraculous recovery might mean that she suggests I should go into college after all, but she doesn't. She tells me she's made arrangements to work from home again today, to keep an eye on me, and that she's going to call the doctor to inform him about my scan and start the process to sort out the counselling I need. She looks exhausted. I don't suppose she slept too well last night, after her row with Dad, the row I'm not supposed to have heard. I see her sad, tired eyes and I want to tell her how much happier she would be without him (and he, her), how much younger she'd look with less stress in her life, and with her white hair dyed, how she could go out and get a good job that would make her feel significant. I want to tell her that I *know* all these things because I've already seen them happen for myself. But I can't. How can I explain that I've witnessed a present/past/future – I'm still not sure which it is – that has seemingly never occurred?

I excuse myself and head back upstairs to explore my bedroom. I am looking for useful evidence: old diaries, photographs, cards – anything that can reveal personal information. The cupboards are full of useless tat that I thought I had thrown away aeons ago: old toys and books and board games. I'm glad they haven't been though, because at least I recognise them: they are *my* old things – the teddy bear I used to take to bed every night, the dolls I dressed and undressed, the Scrabble set I was forced to play with because Mum thought it would be good for me. Just like the primary-school photo of me, which I spotted on the bookcase earlier, seeing these things makes me happy because they let me know that, if nothing else, I share a distant past with this person who's become me. With this girl who's replaced me. There are photo albums too, with pictures of holidays in France and Portugal, shots taken on sandy beaches years ago when I was small and Mum and Dad seemed content together. If I concentrate hard enough, I can still taste the hot doughnuts that we bought on the beach, my mouth full of sugar and sea salt and sun cream and sand.

But there are no recent photos, nothing that shows me who my friends are, or what I've been doing lately. Nothing that helps me now. I know why that is, of course: all my pictures must be digital. Who gets around to printing out their photos any more? And why bother, when you can pin them up and post them, share them and enhance them, or just upload and store them on the Internet?

I *need* to get online. But I can't find a laptop and my tablet is still nowhere to be found. I seem to have mislaid it somewhere in my other life. It's only after I've searched every drawer, shelf and cupboard twice that it strikes me: I'm not going to find it. Dad bought the tablet for me after he moved out, as a sort of consolation present. But if Dad hasn't moved out, or married Tamsyn, then he has never had any reason to feel guilty about deserting me, or felt the need to soothe his guilt with expensive gifts. And so I don't have a tablet. Neither, it seems, does the other me. What the hell did she use to get online? Just her phone?

There used to be an ancient desktop in the spare room. It's still there, I discover, as cranky and as slow and as out of date as I remember, but it still works and at least I know how to use it. As it groans into life, I feel a pang of nerves, afraid of what my search might reveal and, if I'm honest, even more afraid of what might not be there. It doesn't take

72

long to realise that I can't get into any of my own online accounts, because my passwords don't work. I can't even get into my email, or work out what my address is. Frustrated, I decide to Google my name. There are over five thousand results, with pages and pages of girls called Ella Samson, girls from all over the world. I go through them, profile by profile, post after post, scrolling down and pushing 'return' until my finger hurts.

Not one of them is me.

Or, rather, not one of them is the old me.

Every trace of everything I've ever posted has vanished. It's horrible. It feels as if someone has pressed a self-destruct button and all my accounts and profiles and blog posts and photographs have disintegrated into a billion unreachable fragments. The me I used to be doesn't exist in cyberspace. She doesn't seem to exist anywhere, except in my own head.

I'm so glad I didn't have a chance to go online yesterday. I really don't think I could have coped with this discovery then. I would have been destroyed by it. I would have thought about all the hours I'd spent putting up photos, pinning things to boards, jotting down my thoughts and writing messages. Finding everything gone would have been like dying. Worse than dying maybe. Because even dead people still have profiles, and they have memorial pages and tributes too. If there's no trace of you online, you might as well never have existed.

At school, they always said that once something has been posted online, it's there forever. It was a warning: don't post anything you might regret one day. And don't let anybody else. I guess, in my case, they were wrong. I take a deep breath, screwing my eyes up to stop the tears from forming. Look on the bright side, Ella, I tell myself. You're Pollyanna today, remember. Stay positive. At least there are no more embarrassing pictures taken at parties when you didn't realise someone had a camera. No more unflattering photos or cringe-making selfies. No more idiotic comments that you regretted making ten seconds after you posted them. No more permanent reminders of split-second decisions to join fan clubs for bands that broke up years back, and whose names you can't remember. No more fashion mistakes. No more friendship mistakes. And, best of all, nothing humiliating, which you once sent to someone you trusted, that shouldn't have ended up online, but did. I check for it, that picture, in all the places it might be. But it, like everything else, has gone. Relief washes over me. It has haunted me for months, I would have done anything to be rid of it, and now it just isn't there any more, as if it never existed at all. All traces of my stupid decision have been deleted; I can stop worrying about it at last. Not many people get the chance to start afresh. But I have. I can.

The other me seems not to have a big online presence. She has accounts – which I can't get into – but she doesn't appear to use them much and, even though she has plenty of friends (pleasingly, not half as many as me), her public posts are sporadic and people don't comment much on what she writes. I wonder how she spends her time, when she isn't at college, because it sure isn't online. I'm going to have to study her, to build up a profile, the way you'd do with a historical figure for an essay. What other people would call remembering, I shall call learning or fact-gathering.

But I'm not going to do that now. Right now, I need to go out; my brain just can't cram in any more information. And there are things I need to get. I switch off the computer, making sure that I've fully cleared the history first, and go downstairs. Mum is at the kitchen table, working her way through a pile of paperwork.

'You've been very quiet up there. Everything all right?'

'I was just reading. Everything's fine. I think I'm going to go out for a walk now, so would it be possible for you to give me some cash?'

Mum regards me suspiciously. Is this, she must be wondering, another example of my weird behaviour, or is it just cheekiness? 'What have you done with your allowance?'

I laugh. 'Funny you should ask that but I have this problem. And, well, I don't actually remember.'

She sighs. 'Well, I can give you a small advance on next month's. Or, probably better, you could take a bit out of your savings account.'

I have a savings account? This is a rather pleasing development. I can't recall ever having had any savings. My allowance and birthday money were always spent the minute I got them. If I needed money for something, I'd have to schmooze Dad for it. Perhaps not being the normal me has some advantages, after all. 'How do I get it out? Don't I need a card?'

'I can give you your cashpoint card – you asked me to keep it somewhere safe for you. It's instant access. But first I want to know what you want it for.'

'Oh, I might do a little bit of shopping. Some new clothes, maybe. I think they'd make me feel better.'

'I'm not sure that's wise, Ella. You're off sick, not on holiday. You're supposed to be resting, not shopping. What if someone from college sees you?'

'They won't because they'll all be in college, won't they? Staying at home, slobbing around watching chat shows and made-for-TV movies isn't going to heal my memory, or help me get over my trauma. I'll just get crazy bored. I want to go for a walk, get some fresh air. Maybe if I have a wander around the shops, it'll jog my mind.'

'Hmm, I suppose so. Perhaps I should come with you. I don't like the thought of you going out alone.'

'No, no, please don't. I'll have my phone with me. If I feel the tiniest bit ill, I will call you, I promise. And I will be back by whatever time you say. OK?'

She nods, probably realising this isn't a battle worth fighting, and glances over at her pile of papers. 'I suppose I do have a lot to do, and some air would do you good. As long as you keep your word. Be back for lunch.'

'I will.' I lean over to kiss her on the cheek. 'Oh God, I don't know my PIN number, do I? I don't suppose you do?'

'No idea.' Brilliant. She hesitates. 'But I think you might keep your PINs in your phone somewhere, in code.'

'Cool, thank you. I'll figure it out.'

My street doesn't seem as brightly coloured today. That means it's becoming familiar, just like my bedroom and my white-haired mum, and the way I appear when I catch sight of my reflection. These things still don't feel right, but they no longer give me a jolt every time I see them. It's amazing how quickly you can get used to something new, how fast you can adapt. There used to be a tall office block at one end of the high street, which had been there for decades, since long before I was born. It was part of the local landscape. One day, they knocked it down and, after months of rubble and scaffolding, of catcalling builders and clouds of dust, a new, more modern, glass-fronted office block went up in its place. Now, that building, which looked so strange and incongruous at first, seems as if it has always stood there. Try as I might, I can't even remember what the first office block looked like.

I can't let that happen to me.

The bank is halfway up the high street, right next to the supermarket. I approach the cashpoint with trepidation, feeling almost as if I am about to commit a crime by stealing someone else's money, even though the account and the card both have my name on them. My signature is there too, the same one that I practised writing over and over when I was a child. It didn't take me long to figure out my PIN before I left the house. It wasn't difficult; it was stored under 'U' for 'Useful' in my address book – not exactly a code that would require a spy to crack it. Below it was a list of what must be random passwords, which I can try using on my various online accounts later. I'm amazed to see that there is over nine hundred pounds in my account. I feel rich! I have never seen that much money in my life, and I can't imagine how I got it, or, more to the point, how I kept it all in there. On the other hand, because it doesn't feel like my money, I have no qualms about spending it. I decide to take out two hundred and fifty pounds, which is about two hundred pounds more than I've ever had in my purse in one go. I would take more if I could, but the cashpoint won't let me.

The crisp notes don't stay folded neatly in my purse for long. At the gadget shop, I buy a tablet to replace the one I've lost – or perhaps never had – then go to a cafe to set it up with a brand-new email address and password. At Boots I buy some make-up and then, at my favourite boutique, I buy two black tops and a dress. The dress is also black, drapey and slightly asymmetric – exactly the same as the one that I bought last week, except it's now twenty pounds cheaper because it's gone into the sale, a fact that is somehow both irritating and pleasing at the same time. I take it into the changing room to try it on, even though I already know it is my size and that the style suits me. Force of habit, I suppose. I stare at myself in the mirror. From the neck down, I have become myself again but, while the dress fits perfectly, something looks off. I know what I need to do.

From the clothes shop, it's only a short walk to the hairdresser. It is one of those cool salons, its window dominated by a long, purple velvet chaise longue, above which are displayed a series of pictures of models with geometric haircuts. Deeta brought me here for the first time a few years ago, and I've been coming back every couple of months since. I always try to have the same stylist, Becky, because she knows my hair the best and because she makes me laugh. She is in today; I can see her through the window, broom in hand, sweeping up hair cuttings and giggling as she chats to someone. I catch her eye and my mouth forms into a smile, but she has already looked away. She's not going to remember me, is she? In a few minutes we will be introduced and she will think it's the first time she's met me, even though I know her boyfriend's name, how many puppies her dog had, and where she is planning to buy a flat when she's saved enough. I'm getting used to that now, to not being recognised by people I think I know well, but it still wounds.

I push open the door and walk up to the front desk, as confidently as I can. 'Hi, I'd like my hair cut, please.'

The receptionist eyes me suspiciously. She does that to everyone, before she decides if they're good enough to come inside. 'Yeah, sure, what do you want?'

'A cut and blow dry, please. Is Becky free to do it?'

'Yeah, she should be free in a tick. Take a seat.' She beckons me to sit on the chaise longue and points to a pile of glossy magazines. I perch on the end, ignoring the magazines, and wait.

Becky comes over to get me a few minutes later. 'Hello,' she says. 'I'm Becky.' She holds out her hand.

I force a smile and shake it, like it's the first time, when I'm used to receiving a kiss on the cheek from her. 'I'm Ella.'

She leads me over to a styling chair and drapes a hairdressing gown over my shoulders. 'So what style would you like?'

'I'd like it exactly like Louise Brooks.' The way I always have it. 'You know, the silent movie star.'

'I'm sorry, I have no idea who she is,' says Becky, just as she did two years ago, even though she has since done this cut more times than I can remember, and I once lent her a Louise Brooks DVD to explain what I was trying to emulate.

I don't allow myself to sound irritated, even though I feel it. 'Here, let me show you.' I reach into my bag, pull out my brand-new tablet and type 'Louise Brooks' into Google. It brings up a series of images of my style icon. It's comforting to see that she, at least, hasn't changed; she'll never change. She is frozen in time. 'Like that.'

'OK,' says Becky. She runs her fingers through my hair. 'A sharp bob. I can do that, no probs. But it's a lot darker than yours. Want it coloured too?'

'Yes, please, if that's OK.' I used to colour it myself, with stuff I bought at Boots, but it would be quicker and easier to have it done here now. And today I can afford it.

I sit back and let Becky get on with washing, colouring and cutting my hair, while she makes hairdresser small talk: 'Where are you going on holiday?'; 'What are you doing at college?' – that kind of thing. She witters on about her boyfriend and at one point, without thinking, I blurt out, 'Did Jack buy that motorbike in the end?'

She stops, scissors mid-air. 'How did you know about that?'

'I must have overheard you talking about it earlier, while I was waiting,' I lie. If I really wanted to freak her out, I could tell her I also know about his annoying brother who drinks too much, the tattoo he got on his last birthday, and the fact that she's hoping he'll propose on holiday.

It's the weirdest thing to know so much about an acquaintance, when you know virtually nothing about yourself. I watch her closely as she cuts my hair, wondering how it can be that she has to keep referring to the photos and concentrating so hard, when she's created this style for me so many times before. I once saw something on YouTube about 'muscle memory', which means your body instinctively remembers how to do the things you've practised, even if you aren't conscious of it. If that is true, Becky's hands should be able to guide the scissors to create my style automatically, even if she doesn't think she remembers me. Why can't they? And how can I know so much about her, about this salon, when I have supposedly never been here before? Ridiculous as it sounds, I'm starting to think that I might be a sleeper: a secret agent, unknowingly working for a shady spy organisation, programmed with a life story and a set of memories . . . and awoken for a mission that nobody has told me about.

When Becky has finished, she holds up a little mirror so that I can see the back and sides of my head. She looks proud of herself – and she has done a good job, maybe even better than usual because she was so careful, so precise. 'You look just like that Louise Brooks now, don't you?' she says.

I nod. 'Yeah, just like her. Thanks, it's perfect.'

It is perfect. But what I'm really thinking is, 'I look just like me.' I glance down at the floor, which is now littered with long strands of my mousy hair, and feel like I've stepped out a cocoon.

Aware that I'm running late for Mum, I decide to take the bus home. As I head to the bus stop, I sense that I'm walking taller, lighter, more confidently than I did on my way here. I can't help admiring my reflection in the shop windows, not because I'm vain (OK, maybe a little bit) but because it is such a relief to see myself as I should be. It makes me wonder how anybody can have plastic surgery. Imagine not recognising yourself and never being able to go back to how you were.

The display says there's a five-minute wait for my bus, so I perch on the plastic bench, next to a young woman who is talking on her mobile phone. After a minute or so, we're joined by an old lady, her shoulders draped in a bright red knitted shawl. She is hunched over a trolley, which she is half pushing, half leaning on, and walking so slowly that each step seems to be a monumental effort. I stand up so that she can sit down in my place but, instead of taking my seat, she backs away. Then she stares at me, with eyes so pale and cloudy that they're almost translucent, her gaze so hard and cold it feels like it's boring right through me. It makes me shudder. Not knowing how to react, I turn away, pretending to read the bus timetable.

'It's you!' she declares. 'You!'

I smile nervously and edge towards her. 'What did you say?'

'You! I know you.' She doesn't say it in a pleasant, friendly way. It sounds more like an accusation.

'I'm sorry? You must be mistaken . . .' I look over to the young woman for support, but she's still engrossed in her conversation and either hasn't heard what's going on, or is pretending that nothing is happening.

'I know you,' says the old lady again.

'No, I don't think so. Maybe you've just seen me at this bus stop before. Or maybe you're confusing me with someone else.'

She shakes her head, reaching down to move her trolley closer to her, as if she thinks I might steal it. A gnarled arthritic finger reaches out towards me and wavers millimetres from my chest. 'I know you. I know who you are. I know what you are. You're dangerous. Keep away, I tell you. Don't touch me.'

Unnerved, I again appeal to the young woman with my eyes, but she just looks down, as if I'm disturbing her.

'Don't come near me . . . Don't touch me. Do you hear me? Leave me alone!'

'I'm not going to do anything . . .' I begin, but the old woman has already begun to shuffle off, taking her possessions with her. When she reaches the end of the bus stop she turns. 'Don't come after me! Do you hear? Go away!'

'I'm not going to hurt you . . . You've got the wrong person . . .'

Now the young woman is looking at me and shaking her head. She tuts. 'Weirdo.'

'Yes, really creepy,' I say, forcing a laugh. But I don't feel like laughing; I feel frightened. I feel exposed. Who is this old woman and what does she think that I've done? Her words ring in my ears: '*I know you.*' Something tells me that she is not just a batty old lady; she truly does know who I am – the real me. I sense that she can see me in a way that no one else can. She seems aware that something isn't right with me, and recognises that I'm only pretending to be like everybody else. And maybe she knows the truth about what has happened to me. I need to catch up with her, to ask her . . .

The bus is pulling in to the stop. I hesitate for a moment, unsure whether I should let it go without me and chase after the old lady. But I'm late, and she's a bit sinister, and she seems scared of me too, and she warned me not to follow her. If I catch up to her, what will I say? What might she do?

'You getting on or not, love?' says the bus driver, forcing a decision. Reluctantly, I step on to the bus, letting the doors shut behind me. I climb upstairs, walk to the back and half sit, half kneel on the last seat, turning to look out of the rear window. The old lady was walking so slowly, she should only be a few metres away. But there is no sign of her. I look to the left and to the right, jumping up and moving down inside the bus to look out of the side windows, then out of the front. There is no trace.

She has simply vanished.

11

Narnia

As I let myself into the house, I hear Mum coming into the hall to greet me. Still shaken by my encounter with the weird old lady, I brace myself for another attack. I'm sure she is about to berate me for being late. Instead, when she catches sight of me, she stops dead and her mouth drops open.

'Ella! What have you done to your hair? Your beautiful long hair! Oh, Ella!'

Which, I now recall, is exactly what she said the first time I ever had it cut like this, in my other life. If I wanted to, I could mouth her words along with her, like a ventriloquist.

'It's called a haircut, Mum. No biggie. Don't you like it?'

'I don't know . . . I barely recognise you. You look . . . different. Older. And it's so much darker. You've had it dyed too! That's not good for you, Ella – all those chemicals. And hair dye is expensive! How much did that cost? I wouldn't have given you your card if I'd known you were planning to pay for a haircut . . .'

And on and on she goes, until I tune out altogether and can no longer hear anything she's saying. I find myself following the erratic path of a tiny fly as it zigzags along the top of the hall radiator. The fly makes a sudden zoom upwards, coming to rest on the wall, to the right of my mother's face, which now wears a very disapproving expression. 'Ella! Aren't you going to say anything, Ella? Ella!'

'OK, OK. Don't get so upset,' I say, trying to keep calm. 'I honestly think the style suits me better. And it wasn't so much; I got a deal. Anyway, like you said, it's my money. And I can do the colour myself from now on at home.'

She shakes her head. 'I hope you're not going to regret this, Ella. It was rash. Hair takes a long time to grow again. Especially a fringe like that . . .' She seems to think what I've done is a sign of my not being quite right in the head, which is, frankly, insulting. 'You really shouldn't make big decisions like that without thinking them through.' By which, she means, without consulting her. 'Oh, Ella, I knew I shouldn't have let you go out alone today. What will your dad say?'

So that's what she's really upset about: she's worried that this is something else Dad is going to blame her for, that it will spark another row. I want to reassure her, to tell her I already know he will love my hair. He's going to say the style is chic and sophisticated, and how grown-up I look. Because that's what he said when he first saw it. But again, clearly, I can't tell her that. So instead I say, 'I don't care. It's my hair, and I like it. End of.'

'We'll talk about it over lunch,' she says. 'A very *late* lunch.' And with that, she casts a critical eye over my shopping bags, inhales deeply, sighs and walks away, leaving me standing alone.

I take my new clothes upstairs to my bedroom and hang them up in the wardrobe, alongside the clothes that belong to my clone. As I smooth out the creases in the black dress, I can't help wondering where its identical twin sister has gone. Last time I saw it, it was hanging in a wardrobe in this room, tags still attached, waiting for an occasion to be worn. How can an object that I have felt and held – something that physically exists – have disappeared? Has it fallen through the back of the wardrobe into some Narnia-like world, together with the rest of my life? Or did I only dream that I bought it? Is my brain functioning the way it should?

Mum calls me down for lunch. She has laid the table and put a bowl of freshly prepared chicken salad out for each of us. 'It's about time you ate something healthy,' she says, smiling. 'A proper meal.'

Oh God. I don't know what to say. 'Thanks, Mum, that's very kind of you but . . . I can't eat it.'

She laughs. 'What? Why not?'

'Because I'm a vegetarian.'

She starts to laugh and then, realising I'm not joking, stops abruptly. 'Since when?'

Since a few days after my fourteenth birthday, more than three years ago. Deeta and I made a pledge together, after we saw this really shocking animal rights video on YouTube. She only managed to stick to it for three months though, until her mate Rudy tempted her with a burger. I was always the one with the willpower. Was? Am.

'Since, er, ages ago. I don't eat meat, or fish – I won't eat anything that's got a face. So I can't have that. Sorry.'

'A face? It's the leg and breast. As for being vegetarian, I don't know what you're talking about. It's the first I've heard of it.' She seems almost angry now, her voice growing higher and louder. 'Are you just trying to wind me up, Ella? It's like you've had some sort of personality transplant. Everyone says girls are most difficult in their early teens, at thirteen . . . But you? You were lovely then. I thought we'd escaped all that. But first the drugs, the vagueness, the hair, and now this! What is going on with you? Did you wake up yesterday morning and decide to begin your difficult adolescent period now just to spite me?'

'No!' Whatever *this* is, I know it has nothing to do with teenage hormones or rebellion. I'm seventeen, practically fully grown, a year away from leaving home. 'I am not being a stroppy teenager. I'm . . . I'm . . .' What exactly am I being? 'I'm traumatised, remember?'

'Yes? Well, you're not the only one. The sooner you start that counselling, the better.' She whips the plate away from me. 'The kitchen's all yours,' she says. 'Make yourself something.'

I do. I make myself baked beans on toast and eat it silently at the kitchen counter, so I don't have to talk to Mum. Whenever I glance across at her, she is staring at me intently, as if she's trying to draw me out of myself. She's goggling at me the very same way I looked at her yesterday morning: as if I'm a replicant. I turn away quickly, avoiding eye contact.

I spend the rest of the afternoon in my bedroom, researching Jen and Rachel on my new tablet, in preparation for their visit tonight. Like the new me, they aren't very active on social media, although Rachel does have a whole account devoted to pictures of cupcakes. I find a few photos of us together, looking like we're having fun, one of them taken at an amusement park where we must have been on a water ride, because we're all wearing dripping-wet clothes. There's also a photo where we appear to be in a forest, doing something that looks remarkably like planting trees. I can't imagine why or where. And there's another, taken at some sort of camp, last summer, in which we're standing behind a group of young children. The photos stir no memories in me; they could be of anyone.

Then I make myself look at Deeta's pages. Anticipating what I am about to see doesn't make it hurt any less. She has lots of friends, but I am not in any of her pictures, or in any of her friends' lists. She still likes the same music, does exactly the same sorts of things, but she does them with other people. There's no sign that she's unhappy, or any suggestion that she feels she's missing anything, or anyone. No me-shaped hole. It's as if I've all too easily been Photoshopped out of her life, replaced with random extras. So much for being inseparable. I glance at my phone and realise that this is the longest we've not spoken or texted since we became friends. Scarcely an hour went by without us communicating, unless we were asleep. Or with a boy.

Something irrational takes hold of me and I find myself dialling her number – the only number I know by heart – holding my breath as her phone begins to ring, not thinking about what I'm going to say when she answers, just doing what comes naturally. But she doesn't answer, because, as I well know, she never picks up for anyone whose number she doesn't recognise, and so the phone goes to voicemail. I listen to her message, the one that used to feature me giggling in the background, but no longer does, and then I put the phone down. If she ever asks, and I'm sure she won't, I will say it was a pocket call. A mistake.

I feel virtually numb now. And so I might as well get all of the pain over in one go and look up Billy too, to see who has replaced me in his life. To my surprise and relief, 'Will' doesn't appear to have a girlfriend. His relationship status remains blank, and there are no pictures of him with girls. It's all just football, football, football. Was he always that dull? Perhaps he was. I try to remember what we talked about, when we weren't arguing, and I can't.

Using the passwords I found in my phone, I manage to log myself into my own – new Ella's – social media accounts. I take a few photos of myself on my new tablet and, when I have one I'm happy with, I upload it to my profile pages. Then I send friend requests to both Deeta and Will and, before they have time to see them and either add me or reject me, I quickly log myself out.

12

Stranger Friends

At eight, I meet my best friends for the very first time. I am, unsurprisingly, nervous. I listen out for the doorbell and intercept them at the front door, so that Mum can't get there first and say anything to them about my 'strange behaviour', or – God forbid – in case she decides to interrogate them or frisk them for drugs before she lets them in. I hope, pray even, that I will feel a glimmer of recognition when I see them, that I will sense an echo of familiarity. But there is nothing there. They are just people I've passed in a corridor, girls I've seen in a photograph. Average height. Average build. Average prettiness. High-street clothes and, I guess, Rimmel make-up. Dove deodorant (probably, I don't sniff their armpits) and Colgate toothpaste (ditto their breath). Stranger friends. So there is nothing for it but to act my way through our greeting, smiling and hugging them like the best mate I am supposed to be. They seem so comfortable with each other that I feel something almost akin to jealousy.

Not for them – I don't know them so have no desire to be close to them – but for the intimacy they share. Because I don't have that with anybody any more, not with a single person in the world.

I take them straight upstairs to my bedroom, closing the door behind us. I've been worrying all afternoon about what I will say to them. As it turns out, I don't have to start the conversation – my new haircut helpfully breaks the ice for me.

'You didn't say you'd had your hair done!' says Jen, who obviously hasn't been online since she got home from college, or she would have seen my new profile picture.

I touch the back of my neck, where my hair tapers into a neat point, and smile. 'I got it done earlier today. Do you like it?'

'Yeah, I think so. It's a bit like . . . God, you know who I mean. The woman you used to really like.'

I am excited, hopeful. 'Louise Brooks?'

'Who? Is she married to a footballer, or something? No, you know . . . a bit like Jessie J, when she isn't shaving it off or dying it blonde.'

'Oh.' I'm disappointed. 'That's not exactly the look I was going for.'

'Well, I like it. It suits you.'

Rachel appears rather less keen. Maybe it's because she has virtually the same long, lank hairstyle that I had when I woke up this morning, in a similar shade of mouse. Perhaps looking similar was one of the things that bonded us. 'It's not that I don't like it,' she says. 'It's just so different. I'll get used to it, I suppose.'

'Thanks, I guess.'

We settle down in my room, me on the bed and the two of them on the floor on cushions, close to each other. They seem a lot more comfortable here than I am; from the way they pick up the cushions it's clear they've done it many times before, that we've all sat here in exactly the same configuration. I don't tell them that this room is soon to change, that I'm planning to paint the walls and take down the posters. We grin at each other for a few moments, saying nothing. I wonder if they can sense how awkward I feel, if they can tell that I'm not myself.

'So,' says Rachel. 'How *are* you? We were really worried. It's so good to see you. Ooh, I nearly forgot . . .' She reaches into her bag and brings out a bag of something. 'We've brought you a get well present. It's your favourite – Cadbury's Fruit and Nut.' She passes it up to me and I take it with a smile. Good to know that some things never change. I still love fruit and nut chocolate, always did, always will.

'Thanks so much. I'm OK, I think.' I shrug.

Jen looks directly into my eyes. 'Have you really lost your memory?'

'Yeah. I can't remember a damn thing.' I laugh, pretending to make light of it. 'I can't even remember who you two are.'

They both crack up as if I've made the most hilarious joke. What's that saying again? Many a true word is spoken in jest.

'I'm Rachel and this is Jen,' says Jen, playing along. 'Pleased to meet you.'

I wonder how long I can keep this game going. Will it be enough time to find out some useful information? 'I'm not sure who I am any more,' I say. 'It's a nightmare. Tell me something about myself.'

'You're Ella Samsonovitch,' says Rachel with a giggle. 'You're thirty-two and a world-famous tennis player, married to a count.'

Shit. She's being silly; it's not going to work. 'Ha, ha, ha. It's not very nice of you to make light of my misfortune.'

'No. Sorry.' Rachel pouts. 'So what exactly don't you remember?'

'That's just it. If I remembered, I could tell you.'

'You don't remember the accident, right?' asks Jen. 'And what about before that?'

'It's all a bit of a blur, really.' I sigh and then I add: 'It comes and goes in patches.' That's not how it is at all, but I think it sounds credible.

'That's harsh,' says Jen, shaking her head. 'Really harsh.'

I nod. 'Like, I can't even remember how we met. Crazy, eh?'

Rachel's eyes widen. 'Really? God. You don't remember sitting next to us at school in GSCE Chemistry, or getting sent out for giggling by Miss James?'

'Not really. Actually, I don't even remember doing GSCE Chemistry. Or Miss James.'

That's because I didn't. I dropped it. Or it dropped me, because I was rubbish.

'Wow.' Jen exchanges a glance with Rachel, a glance I'm not supposed to witness. It's a look of pity, and it makes me feel horrible.

I fumble for something to say, something to diffuse the tension. 'So how are things with Dom then, Jen?' I ask, recalling the text conversation that I found in my phone.

Jen laughs. 'Weird. You don't remember meeting us, but you remember Dom?'

'Yeah, well, he must be very memorable . . . No, I found your texts about him earlier.'

'Right,' she says, and she blushes. 'I don't really know what's going on. I think he likes me but it's so hard to tell. He's always texting me to find out what we're up to, and I'm convinced I catch him staring at me sometimes, but whenever we get the chance to talk it's like he's avoiding me.'

'Even with my amnesia I can tell you that means he so fancies you,' I say.

'Yeah, that's what I told her,' says Rachel, nodding.

I smile at Jen, the way I used to smile at Deeta when we were having a heart to heart, and hope it doesn't look forced or fake. 'You've just got to go for it and ask him out. What have you got to lose?'

Jen blushes again. 'Do you think? I'm not sure I'm that brave. Anyway, when did you get so confident with guys? You would never do that!'

I wouldn't? 'I don't know. It just seems stupid to keep playing games like . . .' Like I did with Billy when we first started seeing each other. Dancing around, pretending we were 'oh so cool' and uninterested. It was such a waste of time and energy. 'So tell me about me. Is there anyone I like? Anyone I might have forgotten about?'

Rachel scrunches up her brows. 'You've never mentioned anyone. You never really do.'

'What, not ever?'

'No, not really. You've always said you don't have time for boys. At least, not the ones at college.'

I said that?

'Oh. It's just that I've got this vague memory of someone from college. I think he's called Will or something. I have a feeling – a sort of sixth sense – that I might like him . . .'

Jen raises her eyebrows. 'There's only one guy at college I can think of called Will, and you definitely have never said you liked him. It can't be him. He's far too cocky and one of the lads – not your type at all.' By which she clearly also means he wouldn't be her type.

'And what is my type?'

'I dunno – quieter guys, more sensitive. Brainy.'

Apparently, I like geeks.

'But I've never had a boyfriend?'

'Uh-huh. But that's OK, neither have we. Not really. Nothing more than the odd snog.'

I snort. 'You mean we're all still virgins? Seriously?'

As soon as I've said it, I wish I could take it back. From the shocked, hurt look that passes between Rachel and Jen, I realise that this is not something that the Ella they know would say, not even as a joke. Without meaning to, I have just offended my two 'closest' (and currently only) friends, and made them feel that I look down on them. They both stare at me as if I'm not the person they thought I was. And, of course, they're right to. I am not.

If I am sure about anything in this life, it is that I am not a virgin. Even if, as my friends are telling me, the body that I have found myself in is a virgin body, my mind most certainly is not. I remember the first time with Billy more clearly than I remember anything I have ever done: the butterflies I felt when I realised it was finally going to happen; the fear about whether it would hurt; the sensation of lying naked with another person, his skin brushing mine, his weight on top of me. I can recall being surprised at how quickly it was finished, and being mortified to realise that in all my nervousness, I had forgotten to take off my socks. I can still picture them now: greying ankle socks, poking out of the bottom of the duvet, mocking me. I remember every last detail: the clumsiness, the awkwardness, the giggling, the mess, the not knowing what to say when it was over. The feeling closer to someone than I ever had before, but also, somehow, further away, alone and vulnerable. And, most of all, the awareness, afterwards, as I got the bus home, that the whole world had changed for me, and that everyone I met must be able to tell.

I know absolutely, definitely that I have neither dreamed this, nor imagined it. Losing your virginity is not something that you could imagine accurately. Whatever you've heard or read, the actual experience is nothing like you expect it to be. It's not so much about your body, the physical stuff – it's about what it does to your head.

Rachel and Jen are still staring at me. 'I thought you felt the same as us,' says Jen quietly. 'We all just agreed that we were waiting for someone who's worth it. It's not like we've made a pledge, or anything.'

'I know, I know. I'm sorry. I'm not sure where that came from. I'm seriously not myself at the moment.'

'It's OK,' says Rachel, not very convincingly. 'Let's just forget about it.'

'Oh, well, that's one thing I'm good at,' I say, and she laughs. Jen doesn't though, not really. And I think I might just have pushed her away, before I have even got to know her.

The rest of the evening goes all right, or as all right as it can go, in the circumstances. At least I say nothing else that offends or alienates my new/old friends. I am learning how hard it is to converse with people when you can't remember anything that they remember, and when you don't have any anecdotes to relay. It's like playing tennis against someone who doesn't have a racquet: frustrating, and boring. And lonely. I've never thought about it much before – I didn't need to – but all friendships are based on shared knowledge and experiences; who you meet is random, but you click with your friends because you have the same favourite films, like listening to the same music, wear the same sort of clothes, have similar ideas and dreams. You bond over the people you have in common, the funny things that happened at college or at the weekend, the teachers that annoy you. I can't talk about any of that with Rachel and Jen. I don't even have the tastes or experiences that they think I do. All I can do is smile a lot and ask questions.

On the plus side, interviewing my friends means I do I find out quite a lot about myself – about the new me. I learn that I am a really busy person. I have a Saturday job in a local cafe (which explains why there was so much money in my bank account) and in the summer holidays I help out at summer camps for kids. I also volunteer at a local youth centre, coordinating art projects. A straight-A student, I'm planning to become an architect, although at one point I was considering training as a doctor. I sound like my mother's dream. Actually, I sound like every mother's dream. No wonder Mum is so weirded out by the way I've been acting the past couple of days. I certainly don't sound much like the me I know. I seem to have become another version of myself, perhaps the person I might have been if I hadn't met Billy or Deeta, if I'd had less fun – and been less fun – done more work, and had more direction. If only I could understand how. And why.

My friends don't stay late. Why would they? It can't be much fun for them, being interrogated by me, instead of hanging out together like normal friends do. I wonder if, bizarre questions aside, I seem like the same person to them. Do I have the same personality? Do I laugh at the same jokes? Is it obvious to them that they're talking to someone who hasn't just lost her memory, but who has changed, isn't quite right, is a clone, a doppelgänger, whatever it is I am? I wish I could ask.

But, before they leave, there is something that I can ask, something that's been bugging me ever since I woke up yesterday morning. I need to know what, if anything, happened on Sunday, the day before this whole nightmare began. I need to find out if there was some sort of catalyst for my transformation.

'I think I saw you both on Sunday, didn't I?'

It's not what I remember, of course, but it's what Mum has already told me I did.

'Yes,' says Rachel. 'You both came to my house. We did a bit of studying and then we went for a walk in the park. We ended up at Costa on the high street.'

'And was I, er, "normal" then? Myself?'

'Yeah,' says Jen. 'Everything was cool. It was like any other day. That's what's so strange about you losing your memory – it's weeks since your crash and we thought you were over it. And then, one minute you're fine, and the next . . . Well, it's kind of strange, don't you think?'

Is she hinting that she doesn't believe me?

'See, that's what I was wondering about, whether anything happened while I was with you on Sunday, anything that might explain it all. I didn't hit my head again, or anything, did I?'

'No. Nothing like that.'

'You're sure? Nothing happened that was out of the ordinary? Nothing freaky?'

Jen shakes her head.

'Actually, there was something,' says Rachel. 'It was something and nothing, but it was a bit weird. Remember, Jen, when we left Ella at the bus stop?'

'Hang on,' I say, before Jen can reply. 'Which bus stop?'

'The main one on the high street, outside Frank's.'

Exactly where I was today. 'And what happened there?'

'That's just it,' says Rachel. 'We're not really sure.'

Jen nods. 'Yeah. There was this old lady . . .'

I can feel my heartbeat speeding up. 'Old lady?'

'That's right,' says Rachel. 'You got really upset about her, said she was hassling you and scaring you.'

100

'Oh my God. And tell me, this old lady, was she wearing a red shawl?'

'That's what you said,' says Jen. 'Why? Do you remember something about it?'

'Yes . . . No . . . Not about Sunday, but – it must have been the same woman – she was there again earlier today when I was on my way back from the hairdresser. She really freaked me out, pointing her finger at me and saying horrible things and threatening me. But what do you mean, Jen, about the shawl? You said, "That's what *you* said." Are you saying that she wasn't wearing a red shawl? Was it a different colour?'

Jen shrugs. 'I have no clue.'

'Eh? What do you mean?'

'That's what was so weird,' says Rachel. 'You were really spooked by her, but, well . . . we couldn't see her. Or anyone. We thought that maybe she was on the other side of the road, or something. And then you just went all quiet and shaky and told us not to worry about it. The bus came and you went home. And the next day is when you went incommunicado, so we never got the chance to talk more about it.'

I need to understand this. 'Scroll back . . . So you're saying you couldn't see her? Not at all?'

Both Rachel and Jen shake their heads. 'No. Nada,' Jen says. 'Just you.'

I feel sick, certain now that the peculiar old lady must have something to do with what's happened to me, although quite how she fits, I still have no idea. What I don't understand is why Rachel and Jen are claiming that they didn't see her.

They seem to be suggesting that I imagined her. That can't be true. Although I have no recollection of what happened on Sunday (when I am certain I was with Deeta, in my other, proper life) I know what happened today. The old woman was there, as sure as I was. She was made of flesh and blood. She stood in front of me in three dimensions and I looked into her watery eyes, felt her warm, acrid breath on me, and heard the menace in her voice. The young woman at the bus stop – she saw and heard her too.

Or did she? Yes, she must have done. She acted as though nothing was going on around her at first, tried not to get involved, but that's normal. I'd probably have done the same if I were her. And then, when the old lady kept going on at me, and I finally got the young woman's attention, she'd tutted and shaken her head in solidarity with me, and called the old lady a 'weirdo'.

But what if, like Rachel and Jen, she thought there was no one else there? What if she thought I was talking to myself, backing away from someone invisible? What if it was, in fact, me she was tutting at, me she called 'weirdo'?

Could I be hallucinating old ladies?

Panic is rising in me. I jump up from the bed and lurch towards the door. 'Wait here,' I say to Rachel and Jen. 'There's something I need to do.'

I run downstairs and burst into the living room, without thinking to knock. Mum and Dad are sitting in armchairs at opposite ends of the room. She is reading a book and he is reading the paper. They have positioned themselves so far apart, they might as well be in two different rooms.

Ignoring Mum, I march straight over to Dad. 'I need to talk to you about something!'

He looks up from his paper. 'Oh, hello, Ella, I thought you were with your friends. Have they gone home?'

'No, they're still upstairs. But I need to ask you something. It's urgent.'

He puts the paper down on his lap, and removes his reading glasses. 'What is it that's so important? Come and sit down.'

I'm too jittery to sit down. 'No, no, it's OK. I'll just stand here. It's about the accident – my accident. I need to know something about the old lady. What exactly did she look like? Was she wearing a red shawl?'

'That's a strange question,' he says. 'Why do you need to know?'

'It doesn't matter. Just tell me. Was she wearing a red shawl? Was she hunched over and a bit trampy-looking, with a shopping trolley?'

He scratches the side of his face. 'To be honest, I really couldn't tell you. One minute we were driving along quite happily, and the next you yelled something about an old lady, and then you swerved madly, and I had to grab the steering wheel, and then we crashed into another car and you hit your head. It all happened so fast, I don't remember the exact details.'

'But Mum said you told her the old lady walked out into the road.'

'Yes, because that's what you told me. But, in the heat of the moment, I didn't actually see her myself. And by the

103

time I'd made sure you were OK and the ambulance and the police had come, she was nowhere in sight. She probably didn't want to get involved or feared she'd be in trouble.'

I nod. It feels like my legs are crumpling beneath me, the blood draining from my body. I really do need to sit down now. Grasping for the sofa, I half fall on to its arm. It catches me hard against my thigh, and I wince.

So Dad didn't see the old lady either. I have no way of knowing if she was real then, or an apparition. All I am certain of is that it must be the same woman. That's three times she has appeared only to me, three times I may have hallucinated her. Or, perhaps, she really was there, at my accident, and her further appearances are just the projections of my traumatised brain.

It feels like she is haunting me. But why?

And if she isn't dead, how can she be a ghost?

13

An Impossible Puzzle

I don't go back to college until the following Monday. In the intervening days, as I planned, I take down all the posters in the bedroom and buy a pot of cream-coloured paint for the walls. If the world isn't going to go back to normal on its own, I decide, I'm going to have to transform it myself, in the small ways I can. But painting takes ages, and it's boring and messy and stinky, so I give up after one wall and start to rearrange some of the furniture instead. I stand back and admire my efforts and then, against my initial instincts, I put it all back as it was. However much I want this room to resemble my old room, to feel like mine again, my gut tells me it's even more important to keep my bed by the wall. Every morning, with my eyes still shut, I reach out for that wall. It's the first thing I do, my litmus test: the daily ritual that tells me whose bedroom I'm in and which Ella I am. One day soon, I am still certain, still hopeful, I will wake up and my hand will grasp at empty space. And that is how I will know that I am me again.

Time passes quickly. When I'm not making botched attempts at redecorating, I'm dodging Mum, trying – and eventually succeeding – to convince her to go to work and leave me alone for a few hours. Or I'm online, researching new friends and old ones – and myself too – hoping to make sense of who I am and where I fit in. It feels like an impossible task. I might as well be trying to put a jigsaw together with a jumble of pieces from two separate sets.

Each day, I go out walking, hoping to see the old woman, but I can't find her, and she doesn't choose to appear to me. I wait around at the bus stop where she accosted me, watching bus after bus pass by, until my bottom cheeks grow numb from the hard plastic seat. I walk up and down the high street, keeping my eyes peeled for shopping trolleys, pursuing some of their unsuspecting owners along the pavement until I can be sure that this old lady, or that one, isn't the person I'm searching for. Each time, I am at first disappointed and then relieved, because the thought of finding the old lady scares me, and I don't know what might come of it.

Sometimes, to make my search more enjoyable, I pretend that I'm in the pilot for a new TV detective series, *The Granny Hunter*, on the trail of a villainous crone. I know that if Deeta were around, we'd have a real laugh at that concept. Except, with her, it probably wouldn't be a detective series, it would be a wildlife one instead. 'And over there,' she would purr, 'slowly making its way across the zebra crossing, you can see an example of the Lesser Spotted Old

Biddy, with her perm and glasses and woolly cardigan.' She'd try to mimic a posh male TV presenter's earnest tones, but she'd be giggling too much and she'd sound rubbish. I was always better at voices and accents than her.

Was better? I'm making it sound like she's dead. And I suppose, in a way she is – to me, anyway. It's clear that I am to her. She hasn't responded to my friend request and, as the days pass, I'm beginning to accept that she has chosen to ignore it. There are several new posts on her wall and she's changed her profile picture, so I can't kid myself that she hasn't logged on or that she hasn't seen it. Her rejection hurts, even if it's the 'new me' that she's rejecting. On the upside, Will/Billy has accepted my request, although I think he'd say yes to anyone. Anyone of the female persuasion, that is. As for Rachel and Jen, they keep on checking in with me, like the conscientious friends they are, although they don't suggest coming round again.

My nights are restless. I dream of car crashes and old ladies, of being trapped inside hospital scanning machines, of friends with blank faces. Usually when you wake from a dream you know what's real and what's not. But I can't tell the difference; if anything, the jumble of my dreams confuses me more than ever. Sometimes I wake at five a.m., or I think I do, and as I lie alone in the dark I'm certain that I can hear the beep, beep, beep of a machine, but I can't tell where it's coming from.

On Saturday, after some careful research and subtle questioning of my parents, I decide to go to my job at the cafe on the high street. I need the money, I reason, I want to get out of the house, and how hard can waitressing actually be? My boss has been told about my accident so I can blame that for anything I've 'forgotten' how to do, or for any episodes of vagueness or clumsiness. It turns out to be a good decision: the job isn't difficult to master and it's great to be busy, even if I do spend most of the morning on my feet, clearing coffee cups away and wiping down tables. For the first time in almost a week, I don't have to think about who I am or what's happened to me. I don't have to think at all; I just have to smile and make polite conversation and walk backwards and forwards carrying things without dropping them. My boss, Maria, a sweet lady with curly grey hair and a huge bosom, is patient with me and, I discover, I'm allowed to keep any tips the customers give me. It makes me feel good about myself, even – dare I say – confident. Why didn't the old me ever think to get a Saturday job? The truth is I didn't even consider it; I'd probably have said I didn't have the time.

And then Monday comes around, and there doesn't seem to be a good reason not to return to college. I haven't thrown up for days and, according to my mother, my behaviour is less alarming. (In reality, I've just grown better at hiding my confusion.) 'You've missed far too much study already,' she says. 'Getting back in your normal routine is probably the best thing for you.'

Agreed. If only that were possible.

College isn't so bad. Not so bad, that is, if you're the type of person who doesn't mind being stared at and whispered about and treated like you're made of glass. I don't know who has been told, or exactly what's been said, but my 'amnesia' is now an open secret, and that makes me a college curiosity – somewhere between 'weird' and 'sad' on the scale of 'normal' to 'freak'. Rachel and Jen meet me at the start of each day and stay glued to my sides like minders, taking me from class to class, constantly making sure I'm OK. They introduce me to other people who are supposedly my friends, people whose names and numbers I find stored in my phone, even though I barely remember their faces. They say kind things, touch my arm and smile a lot, and several of them comment on my new hairstyle, remarking how different it is, but how they like it nonetheless. There are worse things than being patronised, I suppose.

Once or twice, Deeta passes me in the corridor. The first time it happens, I am startled and I gasp and have to hold myself back from running up to give her a hug. But she barely acknowledges my existence as she walks by, instead turning to talk to the girl next to her, the same sporty girl I met by the lockers last week. The second time I see Deeta coming towards me, alone this time, I smile straight at her and steel myself to say hello, reaching out to brush her elbow with my hand. She stops, looks at me blankly for a moment, then tuts and walks on. It hurts me deep in my gut, her rejection. I'm not angry any more, I realise, just sad. Is the new me so different from the old me, so boring that Deeta thinks I'm not even worth the time of day? How is it that we are not mates, not even acquaintances? I wonder if there's any way that I can engineer some time alone with her. I'm certain that if I can talk to her for only a few minutes, we'll click instantly and become best friends, just like before.

I see Will/Billy too, a couple of times. He is usually with his friends, and I am with mine, so we don't speak. He does smile at me though, and one day I turn around to see that he is looking back at me too. Our eyes meet and he actually blushes.

My classes are tough. I keep my head down, hoping not to be asked any questions, concentrating hard. But even though I have read through the notes that Rachel and Jen have made for me, and I've even spent a few hours studying the textbooks and exercise books I found in my rucksack, most of it is gobbledygook and I feel totally out of my depth. There are, however, weird moments when, if I tune out, if I stop consciously making an effort, I find myself understanding things I shouldn't understand: chemistry equations, for example, and mathematical puzzles. My brain seems to know more than I do, to be able to twist itself in directions I wasn't aware it could go. How this is, I cannot explain. It's like doing one of those magic eye pictures where you have to lose focus to see the image in the blur of colours. Once you've seen it, you can't stop seeing it.

Aware that I'll never be able to catch up – not just on a couple of weeks' missed study as everyone thinks, but on more than a whole year's work – I make tentative approaches to switch courses, but am told that it's impossible so close to the final exams. Nobody can understand why I am suddenly doing so poorly in assignments and tests and why I want to drop the subjects I'm usually 'so good at' and do Film

Studies, when I've 'never expressed an interest in that subject before'. Instead, the head of sixth form tells me that she will arrange for some extra tutoring after college, starting next week with someone named Mr Perry. 'We'll soon have you back on track,' she tells me. 'You'll be top of the class again in no time.' Apparently, I am one of their 'best students'. Nobody in my real life has ever called me that.

By the end of the week, I am back in some sort of routine, even if it isn't one that I remember or can relate to. Living like this is exhausting, and I feel lonely a lot of the time. People keep saying that I seem withdrawn, quieter than usual. I suspect I'm not doing a very good job of acting like the Ella they know. Hey, I'm not doing a great job of being me, either. I think I'm becoming some sort of hybrid Ella – neither one person nor the other.

My only refuge is the art room. There, I don't feel out of my depth and I can almost just pick up where I left off. In the art room I discover pictures of mine on the walls, although none that I remember painting. I know they must belong to me because I recognise my style, the way I slap the paint on in thick layers, my love of bright colours. In the art room, the old me and the new me are almost as one.

When college ends on Friday afternoon, I agree to go for a coffee with Jen and Rachel and some of 'our' friends. It's good to show willing and they're all really nice. *Nice*, that word that means nothing really: sweet, good, kind, with no discernible edge to them.

They're filling me in on something that's been going on at college, and I'm nodding and smiling in all the right places and asking lots of pertinent questions, when I feel my phone rumble from my bag. Surreptitiously, I take it out under the table and give it a quick glance. The message, which I read twice, makes no sense at all:

Are we OK? I know you said not to text, but you didn't show up or contact me. I've been waiting all week. Hope you haven't changed your mind. Text me. x

There is no name attached to the number, so it can't be from anyone in my phone address book. Could it be from someone I knew in my other life? I wrack my brains, trying to remember if I recognise the sequence of digits, but it's hopeless. Deeta's was the only number I knew by heart, and this can't be from her. I feel a pang of excitement, tinged with a little fear. The text is so mysterious. Where didn't I show up? When? Why did I tell this person not to text, and what might I have changed my mind about? And why haven't they signed off with their name?

And then it strikes me that it is most likely a mistake, a message that isn't meant for me at all, but one sent in haste to the wrong number. Perhaps I should simply delete it and forget about it. Then again . . .

Rachel jolts me from my thoughts. 'Are you OK, Ella? You've gone really quiet.'

I stuff my phone back in my bag, and smile up at her. 'Sure. I'm fine. I just had a text from Mum, asking when I would be home. Sorry. Does anybody fancy another coffee?'

14

My Not-so-wicked Stepmother

I don't think much more about the mystery text or its sender that evening, or the following day. I have far too many other things on my mind already, not to mention college work to wrestle with and a Saturday job to do. The cafe is hectic from the minute I arrive, the constant buzz of chattering people and clinking crockery drowning out my thoughts. Briefly, I contemplate packing in college and working here full-time. Life would be so much easier and simpler.

'Ella, see if you can hurry some of those people up or get them to order something else,' says Maria, midway through the lunchtime rush. 'We're running out of tables.'

I leave the counter and walk around the cafe, doing as she has asked. One woman, I notice, is sitting on her own in the far corner, an empty coffee cup on the table in front of her. Although she has her back to me, there's something familiar about her posture, about the shape of her. Trying not to be conspicuous, I walk round to her side, so that I can get a better look. As I take in her profile, I gasp. There can be no doubt: it's my stepmother. It's Tamsyn. Even though she is dressed more casually than I'm used to seeing, her hair shorter and not as sleekly styled, this woman's neat features are unmistakable. In this instant I forget that everything has changed, and I am angry at her, irritated by her presence. I was feeling so relaxed and here she is, ready to spoil everything for me.

Feeling shaky, I walk back to the counter and carry on with my other tasks, while I try to calm down. Perhaps if I ignore her, I tell myself, she might leave of her own accord before I have to deal with her. I stare at her back, shooting imaginary daggers between her shoulder blades, wondering if she's come into this cafe just to taunt me, because she knows I work here. Then I realise that I'm being ridiculous: Dad doesn't seem to be aware of her existence, and my parents are still together. She might look just like the woman I call my stepmother, but this isn't the Tamsyn who stole my dad away from my mum. This Tamsyn doesn't know me and hasn't done anything to wrong us. My fury is totally irrational; it's like being angry at in someone who hurt you in a dream.

I try to pretend she's not there and deal with other customers, until Maria sends me over to her table and I can't avoid her any more. 'Can I get you anything?' I ask, trying to sound normal.

She looks up at me, looks me right in the eye in a way that confirms that to her I'm just a waitress. 'Um, er, no thank you.' She even smiles at me, which is probably a first.

'Right, well, it's just that it's getting pretty busy and there aren't many tables free, so if you're not ordering anything then you should probably settle up.'

She glances at her watch and then at the door. 'Oh, then maybe I'll have another coffee, please. And, er, a glass of tap water. I'm waiting for someone, you see.'

'Right . . . You should really have some food, though, as it's lunchtime.'

She stiffens. 'It's a bit awkward. You see, I'm meeting a friend, but they're a bit late. I hope it's OK to stay here and just have a drink until they arrive. We'll get some food then, I promise.' Her voice is gentle. Not like my stepmother's at all. Every word she spoke to me was wrapped in barbed wire.

I hesitate. The other me would have relished the opportunity to throw Tamsyn out of a cafe and on to the street. But, on first appearances at least, this Tamsyn doesn't seem anything like the woman I knew: the uptight, bitchy person who had my dad wrapped around her little finger and who did everything she could to stop me spending time with him. This Tamsyn seems warm and even a little sad. I have no reason to despise her. 'All right.'

Another twenty minutes pass. Maria keeps me so busy that I don't have time to worry about Tamsyn, or to monitor her. When I do get a breather, I observe her from a distance. Although most of the lunch crowd has now gone, she is still sitting alone at her table, eking out the last of her water. Every few minutes, she checks her phone and her watch, and she sighs. Eventually, I walk back over to her table. 'Can I get you anything else?'

115

She pushes her chair back, as if she's about to get up. 'No, I'm going to go now, so just the bill, please. I'm really sorry I was here so long and didn't eat. I didn't intend to be.'

'You could still order something now if you like. We've got loads left.'

'Nah, I've lost my appetite.' She laughs. 'Sorry.'

I hand her the bill for two coffees. 'So your friend couldn't make it?' It's possibly a bit rude of me to ask, but I'm curious.

She shakes her head. 'Actually, it wasn't a friend. It was a guy, a date. I've been talking him to on the Internet. It was supposed to be the first time we met up. Humiliating, or what? He couldn't even be bothered to text and make an excuse.'

'That sucks.' Tamsyn being stood up should make me happy, in a karmic way – God knows how many times I silently wished for bad things to befall her – but, curiously, it doesn't. I can't help feeling sorry for her. I wonder if this kind of thing happens to her a lot. I wonder if – in another life, in my other life – this is *how* she met my dad, on a date in a cafe, after talking over the Internet. I don't think I ever asked him how he found her; I'm sure that's because I didn't want to know.

She sighs. 'Yes, well, it happens. He must have had a better offer.'

'I think you've probably had a lucky escape.'

'Yeah. You're right. I'm Tamsyn, by the way. With a Y.'

I nod, but manage to stop myself saying I already know that. 'Ella.'

'How old are you? Nineteen? Twenty?'

'I'm seventeen.'

'Do you have a boyfriend?'

Do I? 'Um, kind of. No, not really. Why?'

She laughs. 'OK. Well, take some advice from someone who knows: if you have a lovely boyfriend when you're twenty-four or twenty-five or whatever, don't let him go. Don't think you'll meet someone better in a few years, because you probably won't. Believe me: being single in your thirties sucks. When they say that there's plenty of fish in the online dating sea, they forget to tell you that most of them are pond scum.' She pushes back her chair again and this time she does get up. She looks embarrassed. 'That was probably too much information. Sorry for venting, and thanks for letting me sit here so long without ordering.'

I smile. 'No worries.'

'By the way,' she says, as she puts on her jacket and tucks her mobile phone away in the inside pocket, 'I love your hair. It's very Louise Brooks.'

I watch her leave the cafe, feeling a strange sense of regret. After she's gone, I go back to clean her table. She's left a ten-pound note for me, wedged under a saucer. Her coffees were only two pounds each. It's by far the biggest tip I get all day.

Tamsyn preoccupies me for the rest of the afternoon. When I ask about her, as subtly as I can, Maria says she's a regular, often in here with her laptop or to meet a friend. She says I've served Tamsyn loads of times before and that she's always been a generous tipper. Funny, because it doesn't tally with what Mum said about her. She called her a gold-digger, said she was only with Dad for his cash and that he was an old fool, who only liked her because she was young and pretty. How is it possible that the woman I met today seems so different from the Tamsyn I knew when I was the other me? Was it Dad, or was it me who turned her into someone horrible? Was she only ever mean to me because I resented her and blamed her, because I never gave her a chance? Or is the friendly, sweet Tamsyn just the front she wears in public?

That is, of course, assuming that there ever existed a Tamsyn who married my dad and became my stepmother. Now I am plagued by doubts again. I recall how, a long time ago, when I was a kid, I watched *The Wizard of Oz* and realised, with disappointment, as it ended that all the characters who Dorothy met in the land of Oz – the scarecrow, the tin man, the lion and even the wizard himself – were altered versions of people she knew in Kansas. Her journey to another world was just a dream, the result of a bump on the head when the tornado hit her house. Now that memory makes me question, not for the first time, whether everybody else is right about me. Perhaps there is and never was another Ella, just this one, knocked unconscious in a car accident, my screwed-up brain creating an imaginary world populated by warped versions of people I vaguely know. Maybe Deeta never has been my best friend, but is just a girl I've seen in the corridors at college. Maybe Tamsyn is not the Wicked Stepmother of the West after all, but a single woman I've served flat whites to in the cafe. What if there is no Oz, just Kansas, and I'm stuck here for life?

However hard I try to find an alternative explanation, this is the one I keep coming back to – the most likely, the most logical. And yet, the 'I woke up and everything was a dream' ending is such a cop-out, such a terrible cliché. There must be more to this. Isn't there? I know there must be answers somewhere, and I can't find them soon enough.

I'm supposed to be going to the cinema with Rachel and Jen after work to see a romcom, and I'm really looking forward to two hours of escapism, to not having to talk to anyone or think about my situation. Even though it's not my usual type of film (there's a restored version of *Metropolis* on at the art-house cinema, which I'd much prefer), my life hasn't been a barrel of fun lately and so I crave – need – a good laugh. But when I finish my shift, I find a text from Rachel asking if I would mind giving her a call because there's been a change of plan.

'Jen's really down,' she explains. 'Can you come over to mine instead? She needs some TLC.'

'Sure, of course I will. What's up?'

Rachel clears her throat. 'Boy trouble . . . I'll let her tell you.'

'Oh. But I thought she didn't . . . Never mind. I'll just go home and get changed and I'll be over right away.'

'Thanks, hon. Can you bring some ice cream or something? I've got nachos and dips. I thought, if Jen's up to it, we can watch a DVD later.'

'OK.' I hesitate, loath to draw attention to my 'issues' and then say, 'You'd better text me your address again. Sorry.'

Rachel sighs, as if she still can't quite believe that I've forgotten where she lives. 'Yup, will do.'

It's good to be needed, to know that even though it's felt like Rachel and Jen have been going through the motions with me, I'm still someone they'd call in a crisis. I might not think of them as my best friends, but I still have empathy.

I journey to Rachel's house like a tourist, following the map app on my phone. I don't recognise her street and there's nothing familiar about her house, other than the fact it looks similar to mine, because all the houses around here were built at the same time. Not knowing Rachel and Jen very well means I don't even know which flavour ice cream they like (something that didn't occur to me until I was at the checkout), so I've hedged my bets by buying two huge tubs: one with caramelised pecans, which is my favourite, and a simple Belgian chocolate. Everyone likes chocolate, don't they? I hand them to Rachel at her front door and she thanks me and smiles, and she doesn't berate me for not bringing strawberry, or tell me off because Jen has a potentially fatal nut allergy, so I think I've done OK.

Jen is in Rachel's bedroom, sitting cross-legged on the floor, leaning against the bed. I can see that she's been crying. Her puffy eyes are rimmed with red and her nose is pink and snotty. If she wore mascara, which she doesn't, it would be smeared in splotches down her cheeks, the way mine so often was after break-ups with Billy. I feel sad for her, even though I have no idea why she's so upset, or which boy might have made her feel this way.

She hugs me, and some of the wetness from her cheeks transfers to my ear. Her breath smells of pain. 'Oh, Ella, I feel like such a muppet,' she sniffs.

While Rachel gives her a hug, I tip my head and rub my ear dry with the shoulder of my cardigan. Then I arrange myself on the floor next to them, and place my hand supportively on Jen's arm. 'What's happened?' I say. 'Rachel didn't tell me anything.'

'It's D-D-Dom.'

'Dom? What's he done? Did something happen between you?'

Her eyes brim with tears again. 'Yes . . . no . . . Not exactly. God, I'm such an idiot . . .'

Rachel passes her a tissue. 'Basically, she told him that she liked him and asked him out, and he said he wasn't into her like that.'

'Oh, Jen.' I rub her arm again. 'That's the pits.' Rejection is horrible. I should know.

'He said I must have got confused,' blubs Jen. 'He wasn't horrible about it, or anything. He just seemed totally shocked that I liked him. He said I was a really nice girl, just not his type.'

I look away, struck by guilt. That describes almost exactly how I feel about Jen too – a nice girl, but not my type of friend. And aren't I the one who told her to go for it with Dom, when I knew nothing about the situation, just for something to say? I don't even know who this Dom is.

'Too right you got confused,' says Rachel. 'He was sending you mixed signals. Always talking to you, asking what you were up to, being friendly. What did he think you were going to read into that?'

'She's right,' I say. 'It's not your fault. Boys are never that keen unless they're into you.' I think of how Billy used to

121

hang around me, wanting to talk, always trying to find out what my plans were. And then, in spite of myself, I think of the way he stared at me in the corridor the other day and I feel a weird, but not altogether unpleasant, sensation in my tummy.

Jen sniffs. 'Really?'

'Yeah. Unless he's a hell of a lot more genuine than most other guys.'

This appears to be the wrong thing to say. 'But he is,' says Jen, her face crinkling up as if she's about to cry again. 'He's lovely. Kind, smart, sweet . . .' She gulps. 'And now he's never going to want to talk to me again.'

'Bollocks,' says Rachel. 'Everything will be fine. Maybe it'll be awkward for a few days, but it'll be fine in the end. Just like I said earlier.'

'So when did this happen?' I ask.

'This lunchtime. I met up with him to talk about the project. It just seemed the right time, so I asked him out. Argh.'

I have no idea what 'the project' is, but this doesn't seem the appropriate time to ask.

Jen glances at Rachel guiltily, and then looks back to me. 'I'm sorry I didn't call you too, straight after, Ella. But you were at work and, well, you know.'

We both know what she means. She didn't call me because she senses that I haven't really been there for her, because I've been acting so weirdly, because of the distance between us. Why would you call someone who doesn't appear to remember anything about you? That brings to mind the obvious question: would I call her or Rachel if I needed to talk? No, I'm pretty sure I wouldn't. Then again, who else would I call? For a millisecond, I wonder if this is the time to come clean and tell them all about the other me. But, somehow, I don't think they would understand. And what could it possibly achieve? 'Don't worry,' I say. 'You're telling me now so it's cool. Hey, I think it's ice-cream time. That'll make everything better, right?'

We eat too much ice cream and watch a stupid DVD, which I've supposedly seen before, but don't remember, and by the end of the night Jen is happier. Mission accomplished. It's late, and Rachel wants to give me a lift home but it's only a few streets away, and I need some fresh air, so I insist on walking. Halfway back, I am regretting my decision, feeling cold and lonely and not a little scared. The street lighting is poor and it's so suburban round here that barely a car passes me. I put my phone in my coat pocket and take my keys out of my bag, clenching my fist round them so they become a makeshift weapon. I'm not sure if I'm more afraid of coming across a mugger or rapist, or a terrifying old lady. Although it's been many days since she appeared, I still expect to see her wherever I go, in the shadows, around corners, at every bus stop I pass. Thankfully, she doesn't jump out at me tonight. Perhaps old ladies are tucked up in bed at this late hour, even hallucinatory ones.

Mum is in bed when I arrive home, but Dad is still up. The light is on in the spare room, and I peer round the door to find him working on the computer. He looks up and smiles at me. After my encounter with Tamsyn today, I can't help wondering, unfairly perhaps, if he's looking at

Internet dating sites. I don't feel like talking to him, so I let him know I'm home safely, throw him a casual 'goodnight', have a quick wash, and lock myself away in my bedroom.

I'm not tired. It's probably the result of drinking too much Diet Coke and consuming far too much rubbish food. I check my phone to find a message from Rachel, making sure I've got home in one piece, and send a quick reply. I contemplate trying to start one of the books on the bookshelf – the other Ella's books – but I don't feel like reading, so instead I get out my tablet and surf the web for a while. At some point, I hear the spare room door shut, the creak of footsteps on the landing and the sound of running water in the bathroom. Then my parent's bedroom door opens and closes, and there is silence.

It's lonely here, in this room, in the dark. I feel the urge to chat to someone, someone familiar, so I look to see who is online. Among the few names highlighted with green dots is Will Roberts (my Billy). I let my mouse hover over his name for a few seconds, daring myself to click on it, knowing it's a really stupid idea but feeling excited at the prospect nonetheless. What have I got to lose?

I click. And then I type: *Hey there.*

There is no response for what feels like ages, which could mean that he's not read it yet, or that he's fallen asleep without logging off and shutting down. It could also – and most likely does – mean that he's ignoring me. How humiliating. If only there was a way to delete what I've written.

I'm just about to log myself out when I see that he's typing. *Hey. What's up?*

I'm not sure why I started this conversation. I have nothing to say to him. Nothing, and everything. *Not much. Just felt like chatting and saw you were online late, like me.*

I like chatting . . . as long as you don't call me Billy again. It's Will. Is that a deal, mystery girl?

So he knows who he's talking to and he remembers the canteen incident. That's good, but also kind of embarrassing. *Deal, Will. Although I think Billy suits you better.*

God, what am I doing? I know exactly what I'm doing. I'm flirting with him!

Don't push it.

I've got amnesia. Forgive me.

Yeah, I heard about your accident and your memory stuff. Everyone's talking about it at college. That sucks.

It sucks big time – the amnesia and the fact that everyone's talking about me.

Happened to me once. I ran into a goalpost and knocked myself out. Massive lump on my head. So we're sort of concussion twins.

Two minutes in, and he's already talking about football. I suppose I should allow it, this time. *Lucky us. We're like Mr and Mrs Bump.* I cringe at my choice of phrase. *Did you lose your memory too?*

Well, I couldn't remember if I'd scored or not for a few minutes. Ha!

Awkward! Do you often score? I feel my cheeks redden, even though I'm alone in my bedroom, in the dark.

There's a pause before he types again. *Are we still talking about football?*

My heart beats faster. *Maybe. Maybe not.*

Intriguing, mystery girl.

Listen, if I have to call you Will, you'd better stop calling me mystery girl. My name's Ella.

Yeah, I know. You told me the other day. And weirdly it says Ella above your pic on here too. I just think mystery girl suits you better.

LOL. I guess I deserved that.

So tell me: what was it you needed to ask me?

Oh hell. *Nothing much. Forget it.*

Oh go on, tell me. It's been bugging me.

Really?

Yeah. I don't usually get strange girls coming up to me in the canteen, calling me Billy and then bailing on me. In fact, you're the first.

I cringe. I can't tell him the truth, 'In my screwed-up brain I fantasised that we were going out', can I? Well, I could, but it would read like the corniest chat-up line ever invented, by the cheesiest girl ever to live. And if I say, 'Honestly, it was nothing. I was just confused,' he's going to think I'm a bit of a sad case and feel sorry for me. So if he wants mystery, I'll give him mystery. *It's not something I can tell you on here. It's private.*

OK. You mean you have to meet me to tell me?

I have butterflies for real now, huge great swooping ones. *Only if you think you're brave enough to hear it.*

I'm game, he types. No hesitation. I knew there wouldn't be. Billy is all about the chase; it's the bit that comes after that he's not so good at. *So when do I get to see you then?*

I appear to have engineered a date with Billy. Is that what I intended, what I'd hoped for when I began chatting to him tonight? I have no clue. It's hard to be honest with yourself, when you don't know who you are. Do I want to go on a date with the ex-boyfriend who hurt me, mucked me around and often bored me? That's another question.

Whenever you feel ready, I type.

It seems I do. I'm different now, I reason; maybe he's different too.

Sweet. How about this Wednesday?

OK.

Let's meet at the bowling alley.

I laugh to myself. Bowling. Exactly what Ella and Billy did on their – our – original first date. I guess he's not so different after all. I've never really liked bowling but there are worse ways to spend an evening.

Sure, I reply. *Why not?*

15

Daniel

Monday brings my first after-college tutoring session. These have been arranged, ostensibly, to help me catch up on what I've missed, but I have another agenda entirely. I see the extra tuition as a beginner's crash course in subjects I have no recollection of studying. If, as I fully expect to, I fail to master them, I'm hoping the college will let me drop them altogether. Then, somehow, I will wow them with my extensive knowledge of twentieth and twenty-first century cinema, and wriggle my way back into doing Film Studies. That's my twisted plan.

I've been told to report to room 123 at four p.m. where I'll meet Mr Perry. When I tell them this, Rachel and Jen exchange concerned looks.

'What's up? Is he a slave driver, or something?'

'Mr Perry is a little bit creepy,' says Jen. 'We all avoid him if we can. I guess you don't remember.'

'No, his name doesn't ring a bell. Why's he so creepy? He's not going to try to touch me up, or anything, is he?'

'No, it's not that,' says Rachel. 'At least, I've never heard that said about him. It's just the way he stares. Like he's looking right through you.' She acts out a shiver.

'Lovely. Thanks, guys, now I'm looking forward to this more than ever.'

Jen pats me on the shoulder. 'Good luck, hon.'

And so, when all my other classes have ended and the college has virtually emptied, I go, with some trepidation, to room 123 and give the door a cautious rap.

'Enter,' says a voice that's friendly sounding, with nothing particularly creepy about it.

I do as I'm asked, making sure that I don't entirely close the door behind me, just in case I need to make a quick getaway. When I turn round, I see a small, thin, young guy sitting behind the desk at the front of the room. 'Oh – it's *you*!' I exclaim with relief, as I walk towards him. It's Daniel, the lab technician who was kind to me on my first day back at college, when I was freaked-out and upset. '*You're* Mr Perry?'

Smirking at me, he gets up, looks down at his body, straightens his tie and brushes his jacket with a sweep of his hand. 'Yes, I think I can say that it most definitely is me.'

'Sorry, I didn't know your full name. You only said you were called Daniel. When we met last time, I mean – but you probably don't remember that.'

'That's OK. I'd rather you called me Daniel.' He smiles. 'And yes, I do remember. Of course.'

Truth be told, he does have slightly mad, stare-y eyes. When he looks at you it's like he's performing an X-ray – not in a perverted way, not as if he's trying to see what's under your clothes, but as if he's searching for what's under your skin, at the heart of you. Perhaps that's what I need; someone to acknowledge that the Ella they can see isn't real.

I look away, unnerved. 'So I guess now you know I'm the girl who had a bump on the head and lost her memory.'

'Indeed,' he says. 'Which explains the state you were in that day. We just need to get you back on track, to restore your focus, and that is what I have been tasked with.'

I laugh. 'I hope you're up for a challenge.'

'Puzzles are my lifeblood,' he says. 'Now, please sit down, and let's see what you can already do.' He beckons me to sit at one of the front-row desks and picks up a sheaf of paper, which he places in front of me. I glance at it: it's a test. My panicked feelings about this must be written all over my face because he tries to reassure me. 'Don't worry, it's not an exam. I won't be grading you. I just need a way to find out your abilities and identify the gaps in your knowledge.'

'Right . . .'

He takes his place behind the front desk. 'Just make a start and let me know how you're getting on in a bit. OK?'

'OK.' I bring the paper closer to me and I start scrolling through it. I read the first question, and then the second. Neither of them makes any sense. I can sort of do the first half of question three, but the second part of it mentions a term I've never heard of. Questions four and five might as well be written in ancient Greek. Soon the paper starts to swim in front of my eyes, a blur of unknown concepts and facts, of numerals and brackets and Xs and Ys. I breathe faster, feeling increasingly nauseous, my face glowing hot and my eyes brimming with tears. 'I can't do it,' I say, pushing the paper away. 'I'm sorry. It's hopeless.'

Daniel jumps up and walks over to me. 'There's no need to get upset, Ella. I'm here to help you. Nothing is hopeless. Why don't I go through the paper with you?'

I sniff. 'OK. If you want.'

He pulls up a chair right next to me, perhaps a little closer than I'd like, and starts to talk me through the first question, explaining what it's asking and how to find the answer. What he says makes a kind of sense. 'Right,' he says, 'now I'm going to write you out a similar question and see if you can answer it.'

'OK.'

He turns over the paper and scribbles something on the other side. I read it, fighting my urge to panic or to give up before I've started. Following the rules he's just taught me, I make an attempt at working out the answer and then, nervously, slide my paperwork in his direction.

He goes through it, repeatedly nodding. 'Yes. Yes. Yes. That's the right answer. See, you *can* do this stuff! A bit of practice and it will all come back to you.'

I smile, then shake my head and cast my eyes down to the floor. 'No, it won't. You must be a really good teacher, or something because, amazingly, I understand what you've just shown me. But I swear on my life that it's the first time I've ever learned it.'

Daniel looks perplexed, as well he might. 'Not possible. What exactly are you saying?'

I take a deep breath. I can't put my finger on what, or why, but something makes me feel that I can trust him with my secret. Maybe it's the fact that he's slightly odd – an outsider – himself, so I don't care what he thinks of me. Or maybe I just can't keep it inside for a moment longer and he just happens to be in the right place at the right time. 'The amnesia stuff, that's bollocks. It's just a convenient way of explaining why I don't know things people think I should know.'

'I'm not sure I understand.'

'Yeah, me neither. It's like this . . . OK, what would you say if I told you that I don't believe I have ever studied Maths or Chemistry A-level.'

'I'd say you were having a crisis of confidence. You clearly have the ability. I've seen your grades, Ella, and your reports.'

'No, really.' I laugh. 'It's not about confidence. And it's not that I've forgotten studying them. I have clear memories of studying other things instead, like Film Studies, a course I've apparently never taken. Let me prove it to you . . . Give me one of their exams – right now if you like – and I'll ace it. I'll show you that I know things I couldn't possibly know. I can tell you the whole syllabus, name all the essays I wrote . . . Explain that to me, if I've never taken the course.'

I stop, partly because I've run out of breath, and partly because I'm aware I'm beginning to sound hysterical. My heart is thumping so fast that I'm afraid my chest will burst. *Say something*, I will Daniel. *Please say something*.

But Daniel is silent. His eyes drill into me even more intensely than before and then he appears to shrink back into himself, his eyes unfocused and his body rigid. 'Hang on,' he says eventually, still not looking at me. 'So you're telling me that you have memories of things that haven't happened, but no memory of the things that have?'

'Yeah. That's about the size of it. What I remember and what everyone else remembers is different.'

'And this is since your accident?'

'Not exactly. It happened a while after. I just woke up one morning and everything was topsy-turvy and weird.'

'Not just at college, I'm assuming?'

'No, not just at college – in my whole life. I'm not me any more. I'm a different me.'

I fill him in about Billy and Deeta, about my parents and their 'un-divorce'. I tell him about Rachel and Jen, who mistakenly think I'm their best mate. I describe how a poltergeist has been at work in my bedroom, how my hair has grown six inches – or had, until I got it cut again. I tell him how I served my own stepmother in a cafe on Saturday, and she gave me a big fat tip, because she thought I was a good waitress . . . I tell him how I know personal things about people – like the hairdresser – that I couldn't possibly know, because they'd swear an oath that they'd never met me. I tell him absolutely everything, except about the old lady, because that really does make me sound all kinds of crazy. And when I've finished I start laughing, and do you know what? Once I've started laughing, I can't stop.

133

Daniel waits for me to calm down and catch my breath. 'That's a really fascinating story,' he says. 'Really fascinating.'

I'm expecting him to say something else, to give his verdict on what I've just told him, but he doesn't. He seems lost in thought.

'Do you think I'm lying, or making this up?'

'No, I can see that you are genuine.'

'So you just think I'm bonkers then?'

He smiles and light seems to flood into his eyes. 'No, I get the impression that you are perfectly rational . . . and possibly rather extraordinary.'

I can't help grinning at this. I like being called 'extraordinary' even if it does have slight undertones of 'freak'. 'So what do you think is going on?' I plead. 'I need to know. You're the only person I've told about this. And not knowing what you think is making me feel really awkward.'

'I'm sorry,' he says. 'I'm not one for knee-jerk conclusions, or trite observations. I need to think on this a while.'

'Oh, OK. I guess.' I pause. 'Like, how long is a while? An hour? A day?'

'Well, we have another study session booked for Friday, do we not? We can discuss this again then.'

I nod. 'You're not going to tell anyone what I've said, are you? I mean, like the principal or my parents.'

'No, no, of course not, Ella. And might I suggest that you keep this to yourself too. As I'm sure you know, many people wouldn't be as understanding as me.'

'Don't worry about that,' I say. 'People think I'm weird enough already.'

'Well then,' he says, and he raises his left eyebrow, 'I guess we have something in common.'

The session ends pretty soon after that, which is just as well because I've completely lost my focus. Daniel gives me a set of exercises to complete as homework and tells me he will think on my 'matter' over the next few days. When I leave the classroom, he is still sitting at his desk, deep in thought. I can't be certain, but he appears to be muttering to himself.

Before I go home, I go to the loo and, while sitting in the cubicle I decide to check my phone, which has been on silent in my bag all afternoon. There's a text waiting for me. It's from an unknown number.

It's me again. I really need to talk to you. Why are you avoiding me?

I frown at it and finish peeing, putting my phone away so I can break off some toilet roll. After I've washed and dried my hands, I take the phone out again and study the text. I suppose this time I had better reply. It's rude if I don't. *I'm sorry*, I write. *I think you've got the wrong number.*

A reply comes just as I'm walking out through the college gates.

Don't play games. I know it's you, Ella.

This unnerves me. It isn't a wrong number – whoever this is knows my name – yet I have no idea who they are. Briefly, a thought very likely influenced by the fact that I am now at the bus stop, I wonder if this could be the old lady. But it doesn't read the way she spoke. And old ladies don't generally text, do they?

Who is this?

I receive an immediate reply this time. *Are u serious? Ella, it's ME!*

That doesn't really help much, considering that pretty much everyone in the world thinks of him or herself as 'me' (except the Queen, who is 'we', but I highly doubt this text is from her).

Time to play the amnesia card. *Forgive me, but I don't know who you are. Memory problems from concussion . . .*

Yeah, I heard about your memory. But I don't believe you don't remember me at all.

I'm irritated now. *Believe what you want. Please just tell me who this is.*

It's Dom.

Dom? Jen's Dom? Why the hell would Jen's Dom be texting me? What does he need to talk to me about so urgently? I scroll back through our text conversation but there's nothing from this number that pre-dates the message I ignored on Friday. Did I delete the previous texts? If so, why? And why if, as he suggests, we know each other, isn't his number in my phone address book?

Could the 'new me' be a little more interesting than I supposed?

I'm sitting on the back seat of the bus by the time I feel ready to respond. *I don't know why you're texting me, Dom.*

WTF? Meet me, Ella. We really need to talk.

Intrigued as I am, I'm not sure whether this is a good idea. *OK*, I write eventually. *Can you come to college, end of the day tomorrow?*

I'll be working. And you told me never to come to college. How about I come to the cafe when you finish on Saturday?

So he knows me well enough to know where I work and what time I finish? *OK.*

Please be there.

I will, I text. I just wish I knew why.

16

Reincarnations

Once, a long time ago, I heard a curious story about a little boy named James who was fascinated with aeroplanes. One day, when he was two, he started to have nightmares. He'd wake up screaming about planes that had crashed into the sea, aircraft that were on fire, terrified men trapped inside. At first everybody thought that he had a particularly vivid imagination, that perhaps he'd seen something on TV but his parents said no, that wasn't it, he only watched kids' TV shows. When his nightmares began to increase and become more violent, he was taken to see a therapist. There he started to talk about things that he couldn't possibly know: technical details of planes, specifics of what happened to fighter pilots during the war, the name of a boat he said he'd taken off from and the best friend he'd flown with.

Concerned about his son and disturbed by what he said, James's father began to do research on the Internet. To his amazement, he discovered that both the boat and the pilot his toddler son had named existed. Soon, the little boy began signing his crayon drawings with the name James 3. Then he told his dad that he had been shot down at the Japanese island of Iwo Jima, describing exactly how and where the plane had been hit. Historical documents showed that a pilot named James M. Huston Jr had been shot down at Iwo Jima in March 1945, in exactly the way little James had described. His plane had plunged into the Pacific Ocean and caught fire, trapping him inside.

Although they knew it wasn't rational, James's parents concluded that there could be only one explanation: the little boy's nightmares revealed a past life, the existence of a troubled soul who was unable to rest and had been reborn in their son, six decades later. Even Huston's own sister was convinced. Gradually, as the boy grew older, the nightmares faded. But the family was left with the belief that their son James was the reincarnation of James M. Huston Jr.

I think about this story as I get ready for my date with Will. Although I have been trying not to reflect too much on my predicament, to get on with living life as the new Ella – because thinking about it makes me feel panicked and ill, and it doesn't change anything – whenever I have a few minutes to myself my brain starts to flood with ideas and theories. Often, I'm in the bathroom when this happens; there must be something about the warmth and the steam and the sound of running water that makes my mind tick over. This evening, as I wash my face and clean my teeth, I think about James and I wonder if what happened to him is similar to what is happening to me.

Until now, I have been certain that there is only one Ella Samson, and that the new version of me – the life I've been forced to live in this present – is either a dream or a fantasy, or some sinister plot. But what if I'm wrong? What if there are two distinct people, two separate lives, two Ella Samsons (it's not that unusual a name), who have somehow come together? Could I – the real Ella – have been reincarnated in another Ella Samson, not sixty years later, but just a few hours or days? Are my memories the memories of another person? Is it possible that instead of just having nightmares like James did, I am having daydreams too, and everything has got jumbled up together?

But that would mean this life is my real life . . . and that I am stuck in it forever.

And there's another problem with this theory, one that chills me . . . The first Ella didn't die.

Did I?

Now I am scaring myself. I reach for my towel, too afraid to look in the steamed-up bathroom mirror in case I see some sort of ghostly spectre reflected behind me. *This isn't a horror film, Ella,* I tell myself. *Pull yourself together and focus on the date instead. Imagine how it will go.* Without looking back, I leave the bathroom and go into my room to start getting dressed. I realise I am unexpectedly nervous, which would be a normal way to feel before a regular first date, but of course this is no ordinary first date. It's not a first date at all; there have been dozens if not hundreds before it (granted that few of them were proper dates, rather just meet-ups). Billy has been my boyfriend for several years and I know everything there is to know about him – more, probably, than he knows about himself (he's not the self-reflective type). I won't be spending the evening getting to know him as much as trying not to reveal how much I already know. That, and trying not to call him Billy. Or worse, Willy.

Assuming that things go well tonight, I am well aware that getting back together with him is a really bad idea. And if I had a best friend to tell me so, to discuss it with late into the night, while we went over and over the same issues, and spiralled round in circles a thousand times until she was so exasperated she'd say she was happy for me to go out with a goat, I might have second thoughts. But I don't have a best friend, I have Rachel and Jen, and I haven't even told them I'm going on this date. I almost let it slip but I knew they'd disapprove, or not understand, plus it seemed insensitive to say I was meeting a boy when Jen has just been rejected by Dom. (I haven't told them about the texts from Dom either, for obvious reasons.) If things go well tonight, then I guess I'll have to say something. If tonight goes well . . . Might it? Is this my chance to do it over and get the relationship right this time?

My original first date with Billy didn't go at all well, as it happens. Bowling alleys are too fluorescent bright and noisy and overpopulated to lend themselves to romance. The clumpy flat-heeled bowling shoes made a mockery of my chic black dress and I was hopelessly uncoordinated, sending the ball into the oblivion of the gutter on most of my attempts. Billy was in his element, showing off his sporting prowess and achieving a strike virtually every round. He tried to help me do the same, by standing behind me and wrapping his arms around me so that he could swing my arm back with his, but, distracted by the feel of his hot breath on my neck and the sight of his arm muscles, I kept dissolving into nervous giggles. Eventually, he gave up and decided to kiss me instead. It was a first kiss that was memorable for all the wrong reasons. A few minutes before he lunged at me, he had eaten a hot dog and, as I discovered, the remnants were still in his mouth. That would have been a turn-off for anyone but I had not long since become a vegetarian. It made me gag.

I remember that moment so vividly as I stand at the entrance to the bowling alley, and I cringe again. If it happened now, I'd probably come up with some witty remark to my temper my disgust and to dispel his embarrassment, but I was only fourteen then, and I was mortified. What I did say – 'Oh, that is so gross!' – probably wasn't the most helpful response. I can't recall what happened right after that, or how we managed to get over it to start going out properly, but I can tell you that the kissing did get a lot better.

'Hey, Ella.' Will is walking up to me, grinning. He looks a lot buffer and less gangly than he did on our first date at fourteen, his frame filled out, his face dotted with stubble rather than bum fluff. Although he's wearing a stripy top I've never seen, he looks exactly like the Billy I was with just a few weeks ago. When he leans over to plant a kiss on my cheek I notice that he smells like my Billy too. It's his favourite aftershave, the one I gave him virtually every Christmas and birthday because whenever I bought him anything more imaginative he didn't seem grateful. I wonder who has been buying it for him lately.

'Hey,' I say, swatting those unhelpful thoughts away. 'How's it going?'

'All good.' He steps back and inspects me, the way he always used to, and I feel the same conflicting emotions: the desire to be appreciated and the sense that he cares a little too much about my appearance. 'You look nice.'

'Thanks.' I've dressed more practically than on our original first date, in jeans and a fitted top. The top is green and belongs to the other Ella; I've resigned myself to wearing some of her clothes because I can't afford to replace her entire wardrobe.

He goes to buy the tickets and then leads me to the counter where we must exchange our shoes for bowling shoes. There's a long queue and I have to fight the reflex to hold his hand or to link my arm through his. I know it's too soon tonight, even though it would be the natural thing for me to do. We stand in awkward silence for a few minutes, unsure of what to talk about. This is the time on a first date when it would be usual to ask each other lots of questions. *What music do you like? How many brothers and sisters do you have? What are you planning to do after college?* The run-of-the-mill questions that you hope will spark something interesting, or bind you together when you discover something incredible that you share, like you both have a younger brother (amazing!) or you both follow a band that two million other people like. But asking questions has never been Billy's/Will's forte, and I already know all the answers to the basic getting-to-know-you ones. What I'd really like to talk about is the argument we had at the party, the night before I woke up and everything changed. I can barely remember what it was about now, but it probably had something to do with me innocently talking to another guy; they usually were. This, however, is not the time. This is not even the lifetime.

'Let me guess,' I say eventually, making a pretence of examining his feet. 'Size eleven?' I know this is a bit like cheating on an exam but I'm feeling mischievous.

'Yes. Good guess.' He glances down at my feet. 'Size six?'

'No, four and a half. Sorry.'

He shrugs. 'Yours was just a fluke.'

'Nah, I'm psychic. I bet I can guess lots of other things about you.'

'Yeah, right. OK, what's my middle name?'

This I know: it's Andrew, after his grandfather. But I can't reach the answer too fast. I close my eyes and screw up my face, like I'm concentrating hard. 'I see an A . . . Adam?'

'Wrong! But you're right about the "A".'

'Wait . . . It's coming to me. I can see something Scottish about the name . . . Alistair?'

He shakes his head. 'No! Keep on guessing.'

'I know – I've got it! Andrew!'

He grins at me. 'Right. But third-time lucky, with guidance, doesn't make you psychic, just lucky. You're right about the Scottish bit though. My dad's family is from Scotland.'

We're at the front of the queue now. We collect our shoes and sit down on the bench to put them on. I'm amused to see that Will is wearing odd socks, black on the left foot, grey on the right, and the grey one has a big hole in it. His big toe is beginning to poke out of the end. He tries to cover it up by putting his bowling shoe on as quickly as possible, without undoing the laces properly, and ends up having to take it off and start again. I pretend not to notice.

'So, Ella,' he says, when he's finished. 'Are you ready to get your ass kicked?'

I giggle. 'Wow, Will, you're so romantic. And so chivalrous too.'

'I'm just being honest. But I'd be happy to be proved wrong.'

'How do you know I'm not some sort of bowling maestro? Maybe I'm in training for the next Olympics.'

'Really? That good?' I nod and he laughs at me. 'Amazing. Ten-pin bowling isn't an Olympic sport. Not yet, anyway.'

'Oh.' I pause. 'Well, I'm not a maestro. To be honest, I can't actually bowl in a straight line.'

'Don't worry,' he says, and he puts his hand on my back, sending a shiver of tingles through me. 'I'll help you.'

It turns out that I don't hate bowling as much as I thought, and I'm not as bad at it as I remember being – or perhaps the other Ella went bowling a lot and my arm has learned to aim straight. I manage to knock down several pins and even manage one fluky strike. Will helps me a little, but he doesn't stand as close as I'd like and he doesn't try to kiss me, although I'm itching for him to do so (there are no hot

145

dogs eaten tonight, just a portion of fries, which we share). I'm not sure how much it's him that I want, or whether I am simply craving a familiar touch, to be held, even just hugged. But Billy and I already knew each other when we went for our original first date; we were part of the same circle of friends and had flirted for months before anything happened. Tonight, it's different: as far as Will is concerned, I'm virtually a stranger. And the weird thing is, even though he looks identical to Billy, has the same mannerisms, the same way of talking, there's something different about him. It's hard to tell whether it's just because he's trying to impress me, but he seems calmer and kinder and more mature than he was, less distracted, not so puppy-dog-like. He tells me that he's planning to study Sports Sciences at university and that he coaches a local boys' team on Saturdays. Billy wasn't that together; he loved his football but he loved messing around with his mates or trying to impress them more. I discover that, while he has some of the same friends, he doesn't hang around in Deeta's crowd any more. In fact, when I mention her, hoping that there might be a way to get to her via him, he says he knows who she is but only because they went to the same secondary school.

Will is like a polished-up version of Billy, his rough edges sanded away. We still don't have a lot in common, but I think I like him better. What hasn't changed is the effect he has on me. He makes me feel like there's something drawing me to him, and that I need to be around him. He makes my insides buzz. Billy did that to me even when I hated him, even when he made me cry. That's why, whenever we had an

146

argument, or broke up, we always ended up back together. It must be what they call chemistry. Or is it biology? My friends called it stupidity.

By ten o'clock, the bowling alley is emptying out. I don't particularly want to leave yet and I don't think Billy does either, but it's a college night and the place is about to shut, so we don't really have much choice. We change back into our civilian shoes, put on our coats and walk silently to the exit. Somehow, the awkwardness that we felt earlier in the evening has returned. It hangs like a curtain between us, making us hesitant and shy of one other. And then, as we walk out through the heavy double doors, Will takes a deep breath and makes a grab for my hand. It's both so unexpected and, at the same time, so anticipated, that it creates a surge through my whole body, sending my tummy somersaulting – or rather backflipping – into my chest. Without turning to look at him, I relax my fingers round his, and we continue to walk on in silence into the street.

We stop at the corner of the road and stand aimlessly for a moment, still holding hands. 'So how are you getting home? Did you drive here?' Will asks.

'I can't drive. And I'm not allowed to, anyway, after the concussion. I came by bus.'

This seems to please him. 'I can drive you home,' he says. 'I've got my car parked up the road.'

'Thanks. That would be nice.'

He leads me to his car, a beaten-up old Fiat in a colour I can't make out because it's too dark. Billy's car was a Ford, equally battered; I went with him to choose it, the day after he passed his test. He opens the door and climbs in, leaning over to unlock the passenger side for me. I get in too, then do up my seat belt and wait for him to start the engine.

He grins at me. 'You need to tell me where you live. I'm not the psychic one, remember?'

'Of course, silly me.' I give him my address, marvelling once again at the craziness of a world in which my long-term boyfriend, who has driven me home more times than I can count, has no idea where my house is.

I had the same feelings earlier, when I told Mum I was going on a date tonight. 'Who is this Will?' she asked. 'You've never mentioned him.' I thought then of all the times Billy had come round and made polite conversation with my parents, the times he'd been grilled by Dad over uncomfortable Sunday lunches, and I had to stop myself saying, 'He's the one you think is rude and monosyllabic, the one who spilled ketchup all over the best tablecloth, remember?'

Will turns on the engine and puts the car into gear. He tunes the radio into a station that plays the sorts of chart songs that burrow their way into your brain and won't stop playing in your ears, even though you hate them. He never did have much of an interest or taste in music. As we move off, I begin to feel uneasy, and I'm not sure why. It's that slightly nauseous feeling, the sense of impending doom you get when you know you've done something bad and are going to be in big trouble. I grip on to the armrest for security and try to focus on the song that's playing, hoping Will can't tell how inexplicably nervous I am.

There's a surprising amount of traffic on the high street for a Wednesday night. It's closing time, and the bars and restaurants are spilling out their customers on to the pavement. As we approach the main crossing, three drunken girls stumble on their heels into the road. They cling on to each other's arms, then hesitate and pull each other back, before setting out again. Will brakes hard, making me hold on to the armrest even tighter. By the time they've made it across, the lights are turning red, and we have to remain stationary. I feel a jolt, like we've hit something, and suddenly the old woman is looming in front of us. She leans against the car, her hands on the bonnet and, even though I can't hear her, I can tell from the brisk, wide movements of her lips that she's shouting something at us through the windscreen. Too frightened to move or speak, I stare straight ahead, waiting for Will to say something, to acknowledge her, to put his foot down on the accelerator and weave around her. He doesn't react. The old woman points her horribly twisted index finger at me, and then at Will too, but he remains oblivious, nodding his head and tapping the steering wheel with his palm in time to the beat.

She isn't real. She can't be. This time I am certain of it.

Instinctively, I do the first thing I can think of to make the grotesque hallucination go away: I close my eyes and pull Will into a passionate kiss. He seems shocked at first, almost reticent, but then I sense his body relax and soon he is kissing me back. His lips taste the same, feel the same, and I let the kiss engulf me, surprised at how enjoyable it is,

149

at how fast it's making my heart pump and my body tingle. A burst of beeps behind us announces that the lights have turned green, and we are holding up the traffic. Startled, Will pulls away from me and in his panic to drive away, stalls the car. The beeps grow louder and greater in number, and he curses. I still have my eyes closed and I don't, won't, can't open them until we have moved off. When I do, the old lady has vanished.

'Sorry about that,' says Will. 'I mean, the stalling part.'

'No worries.'

He rests his left hand on my leg and steers one-handed for a minute, until he has to change gear. It's what Billy did, when he used to drive me home, and I like feeling a familiar connection both to him and to the old Ella. We turn into my street, the only car passing down the sleepy road. It's strange how sinister the trees look in the dark, their branches silhouetted against the sky like an old lady's fingers. But I am trying not to think about the old woman, and I won't ask myself why she appeared to me yet again on the high street, or what she was shouting. I'll let myself think about these things later.

I make Will park his car a few doors down from my house, in case my parents are still up and can see us through the window.

'This is me,' I say, as he switches off the engine. 'Thanks for the lift.'

'Pleasure. I had a really great evening.'

'Yeah, me too.'

There's a silence. 'So,' he says.

'So,' I repeat. 'Thank you.' I turn away and start to open the door but Will has hand on my shoulder, and he gently pulls me back.

'You forgot something,' he says. 'We were rudely interrupted earlier . . .'

His face comes closer to mine and the glow of the street lights illuminates his eyes. He stares at me, his pupils wide, and he takes my face in his hands and begins kissing me, first lightly and slowly, then more deeply and urgently. He is breathing hot and fast, the weight of his body pushing me backwards in my seat. His hands begin to wander down my back, to stroke me, to tug at my clothes. It would be so easy to let things go further, to progress naturally, and part of me wants that. But this is supposed to be a first date. We are in a car. And this is Will not Billy; I don't want him to think I'm easy. I really don't want his friends to think me easy.

I pull away, removing his hands, and try to catch my breath.

'Wow!' he says.

I smile. 'I should go.'

'OK. So when can I see you again?'

If I were in any doubt that Will is different from the Billy I knew, this is all the proof I need. Billy was never this keen or straightforward.

'Soon,' I say. 'Message me.'

17

An Appointment with Mrs Sludge

I walk into the house smiling to myself. It's the first time I have felt good for weeks. And it's not just because kissing Will was such a thrill, it's because tonight I didn't feel like I was acting. Will doesn't know the new Ella, so I didn't have to try to be her, or to worry about slipping up, like I do with Rachel and Jen, or at college, or with my parents. I could just be myself, whatever that means.

Mum appears from the top of the stairs and makes her way down towards me. She's in her dressing gown, a long, mauve, fleecy number that zips all the way up to the neck. 'Oh good, you're home,' she says. 'Did you have a nice date?'

'Yes, thanks.'

She hugs me. 'I was getting a bit worried. Did he drive you home, this Will?'

'Yes.'

'So what did you do?'

'We went bowling.'

'And?'

'And then he brought me home.'

She huffs, apparently annoyed that I'm not going to fill her in on any of the details. Why would I? Who gives their mother a blow-by-blow account of a date? If this is something the other Ella would do, she must have been a lot closer to Mum than I am.

'You don't seem very enthusiastic about it, Ella. Didn't it go well?'

I tut. 'Why do you automatically assume that? It was great. Fantastic. I'm going to see him again. Would you like to know how he kisses?'

'Ella! I'm just trying to make conversation. We used to talk about things. This is the first proper date I can remember you going on, so I'm interested. Is that so bad?'

'No, I guess not. Sorry.'

'I'm not having a go at you, but it's very late for a college night.'

'I know, I'm sorry about that too.'

She shakes her head, like she despairs of me. 'I should go to bed. As should you. Don't forget you've got your first counselling session tomorrow. Dad is going to pick you up straight from college.'

I nod. I haven't forgotten.

Which is why, at four thirty on Thursday afternoon, I find myself once again sitting in the waiting room at our local doctor's surgery, this time with Dad by my side. He is trying to make conversation by picking up magazines from

153

the rather Dad-unfriendly selection provided, and pointing things out to me. I'm getting a running commentary of 'Do you like this outfit? I mean, who would wear that? Ridiculous!' and 'This model is far too thin, don't you think? Women never used to look like that in my day,' and 'Who on earth is that celebrity and why would I care about her brother's secret life of crime?' I can't engage, partly because I'm thinking about Will but mostly because I'm thinking about the conversation I had earlier with Rachel and Jen.

'Where were you last night? You weren't online,' one of them, I think it was Jen, asked.

'Yeah,' said the other. 'We were worried. You didn't mention you were going anywhere.'

So I told them about my date with Will and how it went well, and that I think I like him, and that we're going to go out again. And they were hurt and uncomprehending that I hadn't told them before, and it made me feel guilty and wish that I had.

I am beginning to realise that I see Rachel and Jen not as two separate people but as a homogenous unit, as RachelandJen. I know it's bad, and I should probably try harder to think of them as individuals, but I really can't help myself. Like conjoined twins with one body and two heads, they do everything together, have the same opinions, dress the same, prop each other up. If I tell one of them something it's taken for granted that she will tell the other because they don't keep secrets from each other. I also know in my heart that however hard I try, RachelandJenandElla isn't going to happen. They're lovely people but I don't want to be like them. I think on some level they know it too, but, unlike me, it makes them sad and so they keep making an effort to make me one of them. As far as they're concerned, their best mate had a bump on the head and it didn't just take away her memory, it also changed her personality. Friends grow apart all the time, we all know that, but it doesn't usually happen overnight.

Dad nudges me from my thoughts. 'The counsellor is ready for you. Didn't you hear?'

I jump up. The receptionist is motioning to me; apparently they don't announce counselling appointments over the intercom. Maybe they think people will be embarrassed. 'Go to room eight,' she says. 'Mrs Tomlinson is waiting for you.'

I wave to Dad, who is now frowning at the headlines from a three-week-old soap magazine, and walk down the corridor to room eight. I knock and a soft, well-spoken voice says, 'Come in.' On the other side of the door is a virtually empty room, where a woman sits in a comfy-looking chair, holding a blue paper folder on her lap. Behind her there is a bookshelf, filled with therapy type books, with dull-sounding titles like *The Person-centred Approach* and *CBT in Practice*. She gives me a perfunctory smile and beckons me to sit down opposite her in an identical chair. I see that I am facing a window, but when I look through it, it offers me a view of nothing but a white wall belonging to the building opposite.

The counsellor is about my mum's age, except she looks even dowdier than Mum does these days. Everything about her is brown, from her mousy hair to her tortoiseshell glasses, her beige-flecked milk-chocolate-coloured jumper and plain chocolate A-line skirt. She has finished off her outfit with a pair of brown, semi-opaque shiny tights and brown, low-heeled, lace-up shoes. She looks like human sludge.

'I'm Mrs Tomlinson,' she says. 'I want to reassure you that everything you say to me in here is completely confidential. So what brings you here today, Ella?'

I raise my eyebrows. Surely she should know? 'The doctor said I needed counselling. And my parents thought I did too. So I came.'

'And you don't agree that you need counselling?'

I shrug my shoulders. 'I dunno. I'm not sure how talking could help me.'

'The idea of this is to help you find a way to cope with things better,' she says, flicking through the contents of what I guess is a file all about me. 'It's to break old patterns of behaviour that aren't working and find new, healthier strategies to deal with your anxieties.'

It sounds like psychobabble to me. 'Right. Well, I think I'm coping pretty well already on my own, actually. Considering.'

'Yes, of course,' she says. 'I'm sure you're doing very well. I know you've been through a difficult and traumatic time with your accident. But it's all right to admit that you are finding things hard sometimes. Nobody will think any less of you.'

'OK.'

'So tell me how you've been feeling since the accident.' Her expression is so earnest and full of fake empathy that it makes me want to giggle. Somehow, I don't think she's going to understand me. Still, I'm prepared to try her, to tell her the truth and see how she reacts. Daniel told me not to say anything to anyone else but I don't think a counsellor counts. She did just promise that whatever I say is confidential.

'That's just it,' I tell her. 'They say I had an accident. I don't remember having an accident. I don't remember ever driving a car. I don't remember very much at all. It's all a big blank. And the stuff I do remember doesn't fit.'

She nods and mutters something about post-traumatic amnesia. 'Go on . . .'

'I don't feel like I'm me any more. I woke up one morning, a few weeks ago, and it was like I'd become someone different.'

'It's common to feel that a traumatic experience has changed you.'

'It's more than that,' I say, and I tell her all the things I told Daniel. 'It's like I've got a whole new life, which really belongs to someone else.'

'Hmm. These are all common feelings for someone of your age. To feel like you don't fit in, to be unsure who you're supposed to be. Perhaps surviving the accident has amplified them.'

I don't like being patronised. I roll my eyes. 'It's got nothing to do with my age, I'm not having some sort of emo crisis, and what's happening to me is not a metaphor for teen angst.'

'You seem very angry.'

'No, I'm just frustrated.' I look at her, so full of herself, thinking that she knows everything, and I have the urge to shock her. 'Put it like this, mixed-up teenagers don't generally repeatedly hallucinate old ladies, do they?'

At the mention of imaginary old ladies, she looks almost excited. 'Old ladies, you say. Interesting . . .'

'And no, before you ask, I'm not on drugs.'

She smiles. 'These old ladies, do they remind you of anyone you know? One of your grandmothers, for instance?'

'There's just one old lady. And she's nothing like my gran. She's quite mean and scary, like a witch. I've seen her a few times. She had a go at me at the bus stop, told me I was dangerous.'

'Aha.' She looks so earnest. 'And do *you* think you might be dangerous, Ella?'

I laugh. 'Me? Seriously? No!'

'"Dangerous" could have lots of meanings. Perhaps there's something you've done that you feel bad or guilty about.'

'Nah. If there is, I can't remember it.' I stare through the window at the wall and shuffle in my chair. I don't feel comfortable here, and I don't feel comfortable talking to this woman, who is now making me feel like whatever it is that's wrong with me is all my own fault. Daniel didn't make feel like that when I talked to him.

She scribbles something in her notebook and keeps pushing, asking more questions about what's been going on and how it's affected me, but I've half tuned out. I answer in short, snappy sentences, with lots of yesses and noes, which seems to frustrate her. She wants details and I don't want to share them with her. After all, I know nothing about her, apart from her name. Eventually, she sighs. 'You seem very

158

ambivalent about this whole process, Ella. We can't work together unless you're open to this and want me to help you.'

I shrug again. 'No offence, but I don't think you can.'

'You should give counselling a chance. I know it can be a painful process, and that it isn't always easy to talk to a stranger, but I promise not to judge you. Can you at least think about giving this a try?'

'Maybe,' I say. 'I guess.'

She looks at her watch. 'We're nearly at the end of our allotted time. I'll book you another appointment and we'll see how we go from there, OK?'

'Yes, OK.' But it's a lie. In my mind, I've already resolved not to return. And I don't see how anyone can force me to talk to Mrs Sludge. What are they going to do to me if I don't?

Dad clambers up from his chair the second he sees me coming back into the waiting room. 'You OK?' he says, and I nod. 'Ready to go? I don't want to spend a minute longer in this germ-ridden room.' He lowers his voice. 'I'm sure I've caught at least three different colds and a winter vomiting bug while you've been in there.'

Out in the street, he gulps in the fresh air. We walk slowly back to his car together and, as we approach it, I try to recall if it's the same car he used to have, or just another big black estate. I've noticed that as the days pass many details from my previous life are becoming increasingly blurry – what things look like, the order events happened, the exact words people used. I'll scroll through my brain and try to grab at a memory, but it slips away, just like one of those robotic hands at the fair that never quite grasps the cuddly toy you want.

Once we're sitting in the car, Dad reaches over to help me do up my seat belt. 'So how was it, the counselling? Helpful?'

'It was OK, I guess.'

He stares at me like he doesn't believe me. 'Honestly?'

'All right, if you want the truth, it was crap. Pointless.'

He doesn't look surprised. 'I'm sorry to hear that, Ella. I know how tough it can be, spilling your guts to a stranger.'

'How do you know? You've never had counselling, have you?'

He hesitates. 'I have, actually.'

'No! When?' I cannot imagine Dad opening up to someone like Mrs Sludge, talking about his feelings.

'I had it with your mother, a year or so ago. We went along together. Marriage counselling, they call it.'

'Oh.' I look away, embarrassed. I'm not sure I feel comfortable talking to him about that. 'Did it help?'

He sighs. 'No, not really. Maybe for a little while.' He looks like he's about to tell me something, then checks himself. 'I'm sorry to have mentioned it. It's probably not a subject I should discuss with you, is it? Not fair to your mother, either.'

I shake my head. 'Probably not.' But I'm curious now, not so much about the counselling, but about his relationship with Mum. Of all the things that have changed in my back-to-front life, their being together makes the least sense. 'Dad, can I ask you something serious? It's kind of a difficult question.'

'Go ahead.'

'OK. Do you love Mum?'

'Of course I do,' he says quickly. Almost too quickly.

'No, I mean do you really love her? Not just because you're married and have been together for ten thousand years. I know you're not happy – I'm not stupid. I hear you fight sometimes.'

'All married couples fight.'

'Yeah, maybe that's true. But that's all you do. You never talk to each other, or have fun, or go anywhere. I don't really understand why you're still together.'

He seems shocked, looks guilty. 'Oh, Ella, I had no idea that's how you felt. It's . . . complicated.'

'Are you going to get divorced? It's not exactly unusual. Half the people I know have parents who've split. So I'd understand if you did. And I'd cope – I know I would.'

It's not just a turn of phrase; I really do know it.

'Divorce is a big step. Your mother and I . . . we thought we'd try to make things work.'

'They aren't though, are they?'

He shakes his head, then sighs, like he's not sure what to do with himself, or how to answer. 'Things could be better.'

'Do you think you'd be happier if you split up?'

'No . . . Yes . . . Maybe. But it's not just about what I want. Splitting up would affect other people too.'

'You mean me?'

'Yes, mainly you. We don't want to turn your life upside down, not when you're doing so well at college.'

So, there it is, the truth, the explanation: they stayed together for the sake of the other Ella. And that hurts, because they didn't stay together for me. Why not? Perhaps their break-up really was my fault after all. Perhaps I wasn't doing well enough, wasn't stable enough, to make it worth their while trying. They gave up on me, as well as each other.

'Dad, do you think you'd be happier if you'd met someone else instead?'

'Maybe. But then we wouldn't have had you, would we?'

'No, I mean what if you weren't with Mum any more, and then you met someone else?'

He shakes his head. 'That's not going to happen. I've made my bed, I'd better lie in it, eh? Anyway, who'd want an old fool like me?'

I think of Tamsyn, who could – and in another life did – make him so happy. I picture her sitting at home right now, chatting on the Internet to some loser, as unaware of my dad's existence as he is of hers. And, of course, I say nothing.

18

Quantum Dresses
and Gold Shoes

I didn't sleep well last night. I lay awake worrying about my parents, going over what the counsellor said, agonising about what Rachel and Jen think of me, and wrestling with my feelings for Will. When I did finally manage to drop off, my dreams were fragmented and disturbing, featuring jabbing fingers and giant bowling balls that rolled towards me, while I stood paralysed at the end of the lane. At six a.m. I was awoken by a strange, mechanical beeping sound, which grew louder and louder, only stopping the instant I opened my eyes. I suppose it must have been a car alarm.

Tired and crotchety, I drag myself into college, thankful that the week is almost done. Pleased too that I will be seeing Daniel later. Despite what people say about him, I have a sense that I can trust him. Besides, he's the only person I can talk to about anything real, the only person who seems to get me. I know he's not exactly my friend, but he's not like a teacher either, and I don't think he's that creepy. Just different.

On my way to meet him, and already late, I pass Will in the corridor. He hangs back from his friends and walks over to me, lightly touching my arm and leaning towards me as if he's going to kiss me, then appearing to change his mind and knocking his chin against my shoulder. It gives me butterflies.

'Hey,' he says. 'Where are you headed? Fancy a coffee or something? I can lose the others.'

I smile. 'Sounds nice, but I can't, sorry. I've got to be somewhere.'

'You're not trying to let me down gently, are you?'

'No, don't be stupid. I really do have an appointment.'

He seems suspicious. It annoys me; I was hoping Will wouldn't share Billy's jealous streak. 'With a guy?'

'Yes, but not like that. He's a sort of teacher. I'm having extra tutoring. Come along if you like – you can help me with my quadratic equations.'

He laughs. 'Nah, thanks, I think I'll leave them to you.'

I look at my watch. 'I'd better go . . .'

'Hang on.' He touches my arm again, this time with a little more confidence. 'Are you free tomorrow night?'

'I'm not sure. I vaguely promised I'd see Jen and Rachel. But it's not, like, a formal thing.'

'Right . . . I thought we could go and see a movie.'

'OK, yeah, why not? Call me later.' I turn on one leg, craning my neck to try to see down the corridor, where I know Daniel is waiting. 'I really had better go.'

'Good luck with the aquatic hydrations,' he says, and I'm not sure if he's deliberately trying to be funny, or if he's just an idiot.

When I enter the classroom, Daniel is standing waiting for me by the door. Today, he is wearing his horrible brown sandals with white socks, and a green corduroy jacket with brown leather elbow patches. It's like he's picked the outfit out of a catalogue for nerdy science guys. He looks up at the clock. 'And what time do you call this?' He doesn't seem genuinely annoyed, but it's hard to tell with Daniel.

'Sorry I'm late.'

'You can never really be late for a physicist,' he says. 'It's all relative.'

Everyone's a comedian today, it seems.

We go through the homework he set me, some of which I did, some of which I couldn't do, and some of which I deliberately didn't attempt because I'm still hoping to be allowed to drop Maths and Chemistry. After that, he takes me through some new exercises and says he's pleased with my progress. And then he says: 'I've been giving your circumstances some thought.'

'Yeah? Really? Because I saw this counsellor yesterday and she was a waste of space. So it would be really cool if you could help me figure this stuff out.'

'Aha. Have you ever heard of quantum theory?'

'Yes. Kind of. I mean I've heard of it but I don't know exactly what it is.' Who am I kidding? 'No, actually I'm clueless.'

He grins at me. 'It's the way we scientists try to explain space and time. Don't worry, it's very complex and you don't need to worry about all the details. But having reviewed everything you told me the other day, I believe it could hold the key to what you say has been happening to you.'

'OK . . . Right . . . This isn't just a ploy to make me learn more science stuff, is it?'

The solemn look he gives me makes it clear that it's not. 'Do you know anything about multiverses? More popularly known as parallel universes?'

'Like in *Doctor Who*? Or in science-fiction movies? You mean other worlds existing that are just like this one, but slightly different?'

He nods, clearly pleased that I'm not a total dimwit. 'Yes, exactly like that. In simple terms, the parallel universe theory states that at each and every instant the universe splits into parallel versions – one that proceeds in one direction and the other in another direction. Every time you are faced with a choice in life, depending on what you decide, one universe proceeds from one decision and another universe from the other. And so on. It's a little like coming to a junction and deciding whether to go left or right; whichever direction you choose will take you on a different path. There's one universe where you go left, and one where you go right, and an infinite amount of offshoots from them.'

I try to process what he's saying. 'You mean if I, let's say, decided to buy a dress in red instead of in green for a party, there's another universe where I've bought it in green?' I giggle, self-conscious about how girlie my example is. It was the first thing I could think of. 'So at exactly the same time I'm at the party in the red dress, somewhere in another universe I'm at the same party wearing it in green.'

He laughs. 'I can't say that I would have come up with that example myself but yes, exactly like that. But there aren't just two choices, Ella, there are many choices, many universes, each bursting out from each choice made, and from each of those there are still more. In other words, there are an infinite number of universes.'

This is starting to make my brain hurt. 'Hang on – and I'm sorry to keep banging on about dresses, but it's helping me to picture it . . . So let's say I'm in the universe where I've bought the green dress, I then have to go to a shoe shop to choose shoes to go with it, don't I? I might choose black ones or gold ones. Are you saying that, depending on which I choose, that creates another two universes?'

'Yes. And so on. Perhaps at the party in the universe where you're wearing the red dress, a boy whose favourite colour is red asks you to dance and ultimately becomes your boyfriend. But at the party where you're wearing the green dress, he doesn't notice you at all.'

'God, he sounds shallow.'

'Indeed. I'm just trying to make you see how the consequences are infinite. Maybe you buy the gold shoes, and they are slightly too high, and so while you're dancing you fall and break your ankle. This means you have to leave the party to go to A&E. And it's only the next day that you learn that, after you left, someone dropped a cigarette, which set the house on fire. But in the universe where you're wearing the black shoes, you don't fall, so you remain at the party. And you burn to death.'

'Lovely. What a cheerful thought. But then I'd be dead. No more universes.'

'Oh no. You'd only be dead in that universe. You'd still be alive in all the universes in which you hadn't gone to the party. And, indeed, the universes in which you'd stayed at the party, but had decided to go out for some fresh air, or left early, or gone on to another party. Or were wearing the red dress, so were with "shallow guy" who led you to safety.'

I realise I feel energised, that I'm buzzing, the way I used to do when I talked about films and ideas just popped into my head from nowhere. I haven't had that feeling for ages and I've missed it. 'This is fascinating. But I don't see how it fits with what's happened to me. You're not seriously suggesting I've crossed over into a parallel universe? If you are, then I think you're possibly even crazier than me.'

He doesn't say anything. He just looks at me and raises his eyebrows, before taking a deep breath and sitting back in his chair, his arms folded.

'Daniel, is that what you're saying? That the reason I don't recognise my own life is because I've jumped across from one universe to another? But parallel universes aren't real. They're just a theory.'

He shakes his head emphatically. 'Space travel was just theory once. So was the atomic bomb. And gravity existed long before Newton devised the theory to explain it. I believe multiverses are not only possible, they are real, and so too do many others. I can't prove it to you right now; I don't yet have a way of doing so. That is what I am working on in my research. But from everything you've told me, it would be the most logical explanation for your experience, even if it doesn't seem rational.'

I think on it a while. He's right. It would explain why there seem to be two versions of me, the old Ella and the new Ella – the same person but different, living an almost identical but slightly altered life. It would explain why Billy doesn't know me, why Deeta isn't my friend, why my parents aren't divorced – and it would account for all the other inconsistencies. It's certainly a much more appealing explanation than being bonkers, or having a bizarrely selective type of amnesia, and it's a lot less wacky than alien abduction, or being reincarnated as someone else. I like feeling that I might be special, extraordinary, rather than screwed up or ill. But it still doesn't entirely make sense. If I've crossed over to a parallel universe, then how come I still remember the original one? I shouldn't be aware of it, should I?

I put this to Daniel. It doesn't faze him. 'That's what's so interesting about you,' he says. 'Your awareness. It appears that something that we haven't yet identified has caused your consciousness from the original universe to pass into a parallel universe. That doesn't usually happen. It shouldn't happen. But occasionally, it does.'

'Occasionally? You mean there are other people like me? I'm not a total freak?'

'Yes. You are not the first case that I have come across. There have been others. Next time we meet I'll bring you some examples.'

169

'But, Daniel, I don't remember making a choice, or anything like that. I didn't turn left instead of right. I just woke up one Sunday morning, and everything had changed. And I woke up remembering a yesterday that didn't happen in this universe, a whole other life that hadn't. How can that be?'

He frowns. 'I don't know. Perhaps your consciousness didn't awaken at the same time that it came across, but at a later date. There must have been a trigger.'

Something dawns on me, something I don't really want to think about. I say it quietly, scared of his response. 'Could I be dead in the original universe?'

'Yes, as I said earlier, with our party example, it is possible to die in one universe and to be alive in another.' He pauses. 'But I don't think that's the case here, because if you were dead in the universe you remember, your consciousness would also be extinguished.'

'That's good.' I don't want to think of myself as dead, not in any universe. If I'm dead, I'll never find myself again. 'Why are some things the same, like the college and where I live, and others different? Like the fact my mum now has white hair?'

'Anything that's different must be due to something you did or said. You are the common factor in your universes. Think carefully. How far back do you remember this other life? Perhaps the point of bifurcation – splitting – was a long time ago but, for some reason, it's only recently that you've become aware of it.'

'I'm not sure. It must be have happened ages ago because Billy doesn't know me, and he says he's called Will, and we were together for years.'

170

'Think about it, Ella. Try to remember if there's one moment from which all the changes stemmed, and we'll talk about it more next time we meet. Think, also, of anything that happened recently that might have caused your consciousness to jump across. I think I can help you, but I need more information. And remember, you mustn't tell anyone about this conversation.'

'I won't,' I say, and I scoff. 'No one would believe a word of it, anyway.'

I wonder what he means by *I think I can help you*. How? He sounds so confident, almost as if he has a spaceship parked outside and can just drop me off back in my old life, like he's giving me a lift home from college. Is he bullshitting me, telling me what he thinks I want to hear? For some reason, I don't believe he is. I really think he's genuine.

When our session is over, I decide not to take the bus home. I walk instead, going over and over what Daniel said, my head buzzing with exciting theories and questions and ideas, my brain scrolling through my memories like a flicker book as I try to pinpoint the moment that everything changed. When did my days not include conversations with Deeta or obsessing about Billy? When was there a time without them, before them, when they didn't exist to me? When exactly did the new Ella and the old Ella diverge? When did she and I take two different paths?

It comes to me as I turn into my street. I remember it so well, that it could have happened yesterday. Time: it's all relative, you see.

19

The Birthday Party

I am thirteen years old. I am at a birthday party. I am dressed in a short, blue, flippy skirt with a black lurex jumper and brand-new Converse that still look too clean to be cool. I am wearing red lipstick for the very first time. I think I look ace.

Some of my friends are here with me; I've known them forever, since we were at primary school, and we all moved up to secondary school together. We've spent our lives going to each other's houses, having sleepovers and attending each other's birthday's parties. Now we're sitting on the floor of our friend Kim's living room, talking about the same things we always talk about, and gossiping about the same people we always gossip about. I'm not really listening. My legs keep going to sleep and I'm feeling restless and bored. I've been feeling like that a lot lately, ready for something new, although I'm not sure what, or how to find it.

'I need to get up and have a wander,' I say eventually, to nobody in particular. I bang my legs with my palm and

wince as the blood flows back into them. 'Pins and needles.'
I'm not sure if anyone's heard me, but I get up anyway and
walk through the downstairs of the house, popping my head
round doors to see whether anything interesting is happening.
There are a few people pouring drinks in the kitchen, who
look up at me, then go back to their conversation. I follow
the sounds of laughter coming from the garden, but it's too
dark out there to identify anyone. So I head upstairs and nose
around a couple of the bedrooms, finding nothing but a pile
of coats in one room and a couple having a tearful argument
in another. I decide to go to the loo, as much for something
to do as out of necessity. There's a girl already waiting there.
She is about my height, with wavy, shoulder-length black hair
and she's wearing a kind of tutu, with a Disney sweatshirt
and hi-top trainers. She bangs on the toilet door. 'Come on!
Hurry up! What are you doing in there?' She turns to me.
'He's been in there for about ten hours. I'm going to end
up peeing on the floor at this rate.' The girl has huge round
eyes, the colour of olives. I smile at her and she turns back to
the door. We stand silently, waiting for a few more minutes,
and then she turns around again and rolls her eyes at me.
'Bloody hell, Sam! Hurry up! There's a queue out here!'

'Yeah,' I say, giggling. 'I can't keep my legs crossed for
much longer.'

She smiles. 'I'm Deeta. I love your lipstick, by the way.
And the guy in there –' she points her thumb in the direction
of the toilet – 'is called Sam.'

'Thanks. I'm Ella. Are you a friend of Kim's? I don't
think I've seen you around.'

'Oh no, I don't know Kim. Is that whose house it is? We saw the party on Facebook, and it was local, so a load of us decided to come down and check it out. You're a mate of Kim's then?'

I nod. 'Sort of. I've known her forever. School, you know.'

'Right. It's a bit tame so far. Think it will warm up?'

'I dunno. Hope so.'

She turns back to the door. 'Sam! Are you OK in there? If you don't come out soon I'm going to have to kick the door down! Have you fallen asleep or something?'

'Maybe he's constipated,' I suggest, and cringe. 'Sorry, that was TMI.'

She cracks up. 'Ha! No such thing as too much information. I like a girl who tells it how she sees it.'

There's a flushing sound and then the toilet door slowly opens. 'Thank God for that,' says Deeta. From behind it emerges a sheepish-looking guy with blond hair swept across his face. 'Sorry, Deets,' he says. 'I don't feel too good. I think I'm gonna head home.'

'Shame.' She touches his shoulder. 'Sorry, Sam, I can't chat now. Bladder calls.' She dives into the bathroom, locking the door behind her. Sam gives me a mournful look, and then shuffles away down the corridor.

'All yours,' says Deeta, when she comes out. 'Has Sam gone?'

'Yeah, he didn't hang around. Is he your boyfriend?'

'God no. He's just a mate. Tell you what: when you've been, come and find me and I'll introduce you to everyone.'

'OK.'

There's nobody queuing when I come out, which is a good thing, because I've used the last sheet of loo roll. After applying another coat of lipstick, I head back down to the party, intending to find that girl, Deeta, and be introduced to her mates, as she suggested. But at the bottom of the stairs, I hesitate. Maybe I should I go back to be with my own friends instead. Did Deeta really mean what she said, that she wanted me to join her? It's the sort of thing people just say, isn't it? I walk slowly past the living room and peer in to see my friends sitting exactly where I left them, probably still having the same conversation. That decides me: I'm going to take a chance.

I find Deeta's gang in one of the reception rooms. There's about eight of them, a mix of boys and girls, and everyone's sort of draped across each other on the sofas, or on the floor. I pause at the door, intimidated. Luckily, Deeta spots my arrival. 'Hey, Ella. Come over here. Everybody, this is Ella. I met her upstairs.'

There's a cacophony of grunted hellos and then they all go back to doing whatever it was that they were doing, which seems to involve passing something around. Deeta beckons me to sit next to her and so I half perch, half lean on the arm of the sofa. She has taken possession of the thing that's being passed around. It looks like a small thermos flask. 'Want a swig?'

'Erm, what is it?'

'Vodka.'

I've never tasted vodka before, and I don't really want to try it now, but everyone's looking at me expectantly. I put the flask to my lips and take a gulp. It tastes like foul medicine, really foul medicine that sets my throat on fire and then trickles its way down to my belly, making it feel strangely warm and tingly. I try not to cough and hand the flask back to Deeta, imagining how nuts Kim's parents would go if they knew that people were drinking at her party. How nuts my parents would go if they knew I was. And then I think, let them. Deeta introduces me to some of the others, but I instantly forget their names. They're all really friendly, though, and the more swigs I have, the more relaxed and part of their crowd I feel.

'Hey, it's Ella, right?' One of the girls is talking to me. 'Deeta says you know the person whose house this is. Can you ask them to change the music?'

I stumble to my feet. My head swims and I giggle. 'OK, sure, what do you want her to put on?'

'This,' says Deeta, and I notice that a CD is floating under my nose. It doesn't have a proper cover.

'What is it?'

Deeta looks pleased with herself. 'It's a demo by an up-and-coming band called The Wonderfulls. My brother says they're going to be huge. He knows the bass player.'

I don't remember asking Kim to change the music but somehow the CD is playing, and it's loud, and I like it, and everyone starts dancing. And suddenly there seem to be about a hundred people in the downstairs of the house, and you can hardly walk from room to room. And then I'm in the living room, and I realise that all the friends I came with have gone home, but I don't care, and Deeta is *grabbing my arm and dancing with me, and there's loads of boys around us, and one of them keeps looking at me. And I keep looking at him too.*

I am thirteen years old and I am at a party, and I have absolutely no idea that tonight will change the course of my life. As I drink and chat and laugh and dance with a group of strangers, I am unaware that I have just met the girl who will soon become my best friend and the boy who will be my first boyfriend. I certainly have no inkling that by making the choices I did tonight, that simply by being here, I have diverted my life on to a different path. I have created a new universe, in which there will be a new me.

It's probably a very good thing that I don't know any of this, or I would spontaneously combust.

I know it now, today, at seventeen, however. I am certain of it. There's just one thing I need to do to prove it. As soon as I'm home, I log on to instant messaging and find Kim's name. She's not at my college and I can't remember the last time I saw her or spoke to her, in any universe.

Hi Kim, do you remember me? It's Ella Samson.

She's not online and my message floats there, unanswered, while I have my dinner and do my homework. It remains on my screen, neglected and ignored, long after I've chatted to Rachel and Jen and made arrangements to see Will tomorrow night. Finally, at ten o'clock, just when I am about to give up and log off, I notice that there's a response.

Ella? From school?

She's still online. I type quickly. *Yes, that's me. You well?*

177

I'm fine. This is a surprise. What have you been up to?

I know it's mean, but I don't really want to catch up with her. This is not an attempt to reignite a long-lost friendship; there's something I need to know. Or rather, to confirm. *This and that. All good. Look, I know we probably haven't spoken properly for ages, and this is going to sound like a weird question, but did you happen to have a party for your fourteenth birthday? A house party?*

Yes. Why on earth do you want to know that now?

It's not important. Were there a load of gatecrashers at this party, people who found out about it on Facebook?

Oh God, yes. Don't remind me. I got into tons of trouble with my parents. There were fag burns in the carpet and stuff got broken, and people were drinking and they threw up everywhere. I got grounded for ages afterwards. Why do you want to know?

No reason. It's for a project I'm working on at college. Social media stuff. Don't worry about it.

OK . . .

So what I really want to know is this: can you remember if I was there?

God, what a weird thing to ask. Don't you remember? I don't know. Let me think. Hang on, I'll go through my photos. I'll be right back.

I wait while she hunts for her pictures, watching the cursor blink the seconds away, holding my breath. If I'm right, I know what she is going to say.

No, you're not in any of the pictures. That's right – I have a vague memory that you were supposed to come but you didn't feel well, or something. Everyone else from school was there but you didn't make it. Does that help?

Yes, I type, as all around me a billion, trillion, infinite and infinitesimal universes explode and die. *It helps a lot. Thank you.*

20

An All-Powerful
Creator of Universes

Should I turn left or right? Which clothes should I pick from the wardrobe? Would it be better to have jam or peanut butter on my toast? Since Daniel told me his theory yesterday, nothing has been quite the same. I am now conscious of every tiny choice I make, and the fact that they all have unforeseen consequences, not just for me, but for others too. When I look at my hands I no longer see mere fingers, but wands shooting out magic laser beams that create new worlds with everything they touch. When I peer into the mirror I can see myself reflected an infinite number of times, each face representing another version of me. (And that makes putting on my mascara really tricky, I can tell you.) Even just getting out of bed this morning took forever because I worried that if I put my left foot down first, rather than my right foot, it would alter the future. By the time I'd decided that this minuscule decision probably didn't matter, I was running late for work.

My awareness that I am an all-powerful creator of universes is, ironically and contrarily, making me a bit useless: slow and indecisive and clumsy. In the cafe I worry about whether I should serve this woman before that man, or whose plate I should tidy away first. When Tamsyn pops in briefly with a friend to buy a takeaway coffee, I forget to ask if she'd like chocolate powder sprinkled on her cappuccino because I'm too busy staring at her, thinking, 'If I had gone to that fourteenth birthday party and made new friends, and gone off the rails, you'd be married to my father right now. You're single because of ME.' Maria notices how distracted I am and asks if I'm OK. I tell her I didn't sleep too well last night, which is actually true. How can you sleep when you know you're awake in an infinite number of other universes?

There's so much going on in my head that I've barely had time to think about my meeting with Dom. As Saturday afternoon progresses, however, my nerves begin to prickle at me. Perhaps it was stupid to agree to meet him at the cafe because now I'm trapped here, unable to change my mind or escape, and there are so many guys walking in and out that when he finally does arrive, I won't have a clue which of them is him. Why he wants to see me at all is a mystery – let alone why it's so important to him. Naturally, I tried to find out about him online but, without a surname, or any real details to go on, it was impossible. He wasn't in Rachel's or Jen's friends lists and I couldn't ask them, the only two people who might be able to tell me, because there's something so cloak and dagger about this meeting, about his contact with me. So, here I am, keeping a big secret when I'm not sure why, or who I'm protecting. It could be Dom, it could be Rachel and Jen, and it could just as likely be myself.

It's funny how when you've never met someone you have this idea of how they'll look, just based on their name and what they've said and done, and on all the other people with that name you've come across in your life. It's a bit like picturing a character in a book that you're reading; seeing the film version is often disappointing because they cast someone who looks all wrong, who doesn't match up to the image in your head. When Dom comes into the cafe I don't clock that it's him at first, because the guy he turns out to be is shorter than I'm expecting, and looks older too. I imagined someone my age, but he must be at least twenty. I notice that he has lovely blue eyes, which are hidden behind black-framed round glasses, and a slightly gap-toothed smile. I wouldn't say he's good-looking, at least not in a conventional way, but there's definitely something attractive about him. I can see why Jen was so keen. He kisses me hello, which feels too familiar, because as far as I'm concerned it's the first time we've met. Then again, it's normal to kiss strangers hello in countries like France, isn't it?

'It's so good to see you, Ella,' he says. 'You look great. I love your haircut – I almost didn't recognise you.'

I'm not sure how to respond, so I just nod and attempt a smile. 'Take a seat and I'll get you a coffee,' I say, without asking if he wants one. Although I'm not officially on duty any more, Maria doesn't mind if I help myself to the odd cup after work. I bring two cappuccinos back to the table and sit down opposite him. 'It's on the house.'

'Thanks. Well, this is all a bit weird,' he says, nursing his mug.

'Tell me about it.'

'I can tell by the way you're staring at me that you really don't remember anything about me, do you?'

'No, I'm sorry. I'm not lying to you.'

'Yes, I know that. Jen told me what had happened, about the accident and the concussion and everything. I only agreed to meet her the other day because I needed to know why you'd disappeared and what was going on with you. I wasn't expecting her to declare her undying love and ask me out. That was kind of awkward.'

'Oh. Whoops. She really likes you. She was really hurt you rejected her.'

He shrugs. 'I know. I'm sorry I upset her but she got the wrong idea. Anyway, forget about Jen. I'm here to see you. And I guess I was just hoping something might come back to you when you saw me.' He laughs. 'This isn't great for the old ego, you know. Actually, it's a bit gutting.'

'I'm sorry. If it helps, I've had the same thing happen to me,' I say, thinking of the look on Deeta's face when I tried to connect with her. 'It sucks. So, now you're here, why did you want to meet me? And why all the secrecy?'

He sighs. 'That was down to you, not me. You're the one who asked me never to text you first, or to call you unless you said it was safe. I was being respectful.'

'Oh? Why would I do that?'

He looks down at the table, like he's suddenly shy. 'A few reasons. Partly because of my age . . .'

'Your age?' I study him for wrinkles and grey hairs. 'How old exactly are you?'

He squirms in his seat. 'I'm only twenty-one. But you thought I was too old . . . or that your parents would think it.'

'Too old for what?'

He slams down his coffee cup in frustration. 'Jeez, Ella, you never used to be this slow on the uptake. This is horrible.' He can't look at me. 'What do you think I mean? We had started seeing each other, OK? Dating. I was your boyfriend.'

'Oh. Oh? Oh.' That possibility had not even occurred to me. I stare at him, trying to imagine kissing this complete stranger, being held by him. I can't. Boyfriend? Secret boyfriend? The other Ella is certainly full of surprises. 'But . . . but . . . Jen and Rachel said I didn't have a boyfriend.'

'That's because they don't know about us. We hid it from them, because of Jen's crush on me. You didn't want to hurt her. Honour among friends or something.'

It strikes me that he could be lying. If nobody else knows about our 'relationship', how do I know that I can trust what he says? Yet he sounds authentic and, more pertinently, why the hell would he lie? Not unless he's some sort of masochist who enjoys being rejected and humiliated in cafes. 'Right. That does make sense. Wow. God. This is weird. So how long had we been seeing each other for?'

'Not long, if I'm honest. We'd only been on a couple of dates. We were supposed to have a third but, well, you

184

didn't turn up. "I can't remember who the hell you are" sure beats "It's not you, it's me" in the list of top ten break-up excuses. You're a true original, Ella.'

'Yeah. Sorry, again. Please will you remind me how we know each other? You're obviously not at my college.'

'Through the hospice project.' He registers the look of puzzlement on my face. 'You don't remember that either? We were all volunteers at St Martha's – you, me, Jen and Rachel. We've known each other for a few months. You were doing some artwork for the children's bedrooms; we were doing it together. That's how we got close. I'm a Fine Arts student.'

'Really? I was?' This never came up in conversation with Rachel or Jen. I have to stop myself from saying, 'What a lovely thing to do.' I'm once again humbled by how much nicer a person the other Ella is than me, and amazed at how she manages to fit so much into her time. What did I do, apart from hang out with Deeta and Billy, go shopping and watch YouTube videos and old movies? I grin, in spite of myself, basking in the reflected glory.

'Yes. You were pretty good at it too. I'll take you to show you what you did, if you like.'

'Er, yeah, OK. Some other time, maybe.'

'Yeah, sorry, I didn't mean right now. That was probably a bit previous of me, with you thinking that we've only just met and all. Here, let me show you something. It might help.' He pulls his phone out of his jacket pocket, fiddles with it and passes it over to me. 'Read these. I know you delete all my texts, but I don't delete yours.'

I take the phone and start to scroll through. There are lots of messages from 'Ella S', friendly messages that become increasingly flirty and peppered with innuendo. They make me blush. They also make me feel like I'm cheating on Will. I hand back the phone. 'I'm sorry but I don't remember writing them. I'm a bit weirded out to be honest. And I really should get going.'

'Oh,' he says. 'I didn't mean to freak you out. I was hoping we could spend a bit of time together, catching up. I've been waiting for weeks.'

'I really can't. I'm busy tonight.'

'With Rachel and Jen?'

'Actually, no.' It comes out without thinking, and I cringe at my honesty. I should just have lied and agreed.

'With another guy?'

I nod. 'Yeah, I'm really sorry. But I didn't know . . .'

I can't read his expression. I think he's really hurt, but trying not to show it. 'First date?'

'Second actually. Sort of.'

'So it's early days and I still have a chance, then?' He laughs, although he doesn't look like he's finding much humour in the situation. 'Look, we could meet tomorrow afternoon instead, if you like, and if you're free. I just want the chance to spend some time with you, so you can get to know me again. Well, until your memory comes back. Just as friends, obviously. It's totally up to you.'

'OK. I guess it wouldn't do any harm.'

'So are you?'

'What?'

'Free tomorrow.'

'Yeah, I think so.'

'Why don't we meet at the British Museum? It's where we were supposed to meet the other week. You wanted to see the mummies. Three o'clock?'

The British Museum? Mummies? It's not a place I've ever gone to, or thought of going to. It is, in fact, the sort of place my parents would drag me round at weekends when I was younger, so they didn't have to talk to each other. 'OK,' I say, bemused. 'I'll meet you there. Probably best if we travel in separately, so no one sees us.' I stand up. 'It was nice to . . . Bye then. Till tomorrow.'

He jumps to his feet. 'At least let me walk you to the bus stop. Otherwise it feels like we've just had a business meeting.'

'Yeah, all right. I'll just get my coat and bag from the back.'

Outside on the high street the shops are discharging their final customers and the pavements are crammed with people and their shopping bags. I walk alongside Dom, trying to maintain a comfortable distance between us, but we keep being jostled and knocking into each other. As we're both so polite and English this means that our entire conversation ends up as string of sorrys interspersed with awkward silences. I do wish he'd let me walk to the bus stop alone.

We're almost there when something catches my eye, and I freeze. It's *her*. She's on the other side of the road this time but there's no mistaking her: wizened and shrivelled and as old as the grave. She has on the same red shawl and I know her shuffling gait.

'What is it? What's wrong?' asks Dom. 'Why have you stopped?'

'It's nothing. Ignore me.' I rub my eyes, trying to make the image go away, but it doesn't work.

'You look totally spooked. You've gone white. What's up? Tell me. You can trust me.'

I shake my head. 'You're going to think I'm seriously crazy.'

'No, I won't, I promise. Just tell me . . .'

'Yes you will. I've just seen this old lady . . . I keep seeing her. She scares me a bit.'

'What? Which old lady?'

I point my finger at the apparition. 'She has a red shawl and a shopping trolley. Like she always does. My brain's been doing weird things since my accident. She'll disappear in a minute.'

Dom stands next to me and looks out across the traffic. 'What are you on about? That old lady? Over the road? The tiny one, who's bent over with her bags?'

'Wait! You can see her?'

He laughs. 'Yes, of course I can see her. I'm not that short-sighted; the glasses are more for image than necessity. She looks harmless enough. Why are you scared of her?'

He can see her? She's real? She's not a hallucination? How can this be? Does Dom share whatever sickness it is that I have – or has she been real all along? Perhaps it's not me; perhaps everybody else has been blind. Or worse, maybe they have been pretending that she isn't there to make me think I'm losing my mind.

'Sorry, but I need to talk to her,' I say, spinning round and doubling back on myself. 'Go home if you like!'

The pedestrian crossing isn't far, and the old woman is going so slowly I should be able to catch her up. I wait for a gap in the traffic, but it keeps on coming, and the lights are taking forever to change. Eventually, I take my chance and dart into the road. A car horn blares and I feel a hand on my arm, dragging me back. Dom is by my side again. My heart is beating so fast I can hear the blood pumping in my ears.

'What the hell are you doing?' he says. He sounds angry. 'Whatever it is, it's not worth getting yourself killed for.'

'If she's real, I need to talk to her.'

'OK, OK. Look, the lights are changing now, so you can do it without dying.'

I'm not listening to him; I'm already running across the road, my focus not on the lights or the traffic but on the old lady, who is beginning to disappear out of view into the swarm of pedestrians. Thank goodness she wears red, when everyone else seems to favour black or grey. When I'm almost upon her, walking right next to her, I slow down my pace and try to catch my breath, to think through what I'm going to say. What exactly am I going to say? *Are you real? Why do you keep scaring the hell out of me?*

'Excuse me!'

She doesn't respond. Might she be deaf, or is she unable to see *me*, in the same way that Dad and Billy and Rachel and Jen couldn't see her? I reach out and put my hand on her shoulder. It's cold, bony, but definitely living human; I snatch my hand away again. 'Excuse me. I need to talk to you.'

She is walking so slowly she barely needs to slow down in order to come to a complete stop. She peers up at me and it seems to me that a sliver of light passes across her cloudy eyes. Then it's gone again and I think it must just have been a reflection from the passing traffic.

'Hello, dear.' She smiles, but it looks like she's smiling at someone else, someone I can't see. 'I'm going to be very late. I think you should come back another day.'

'No, no.' I'm conscious that Dom is, annoyingly, by my side again, but I ignore him. 'You don't understand. I need to talk to you. About an accident. About whether you know me.'

'Has there been an accident? Oh dear. Then you should call the police, dearie.'

'No . . . I think we were involved in an accident. You and I. Last month. And I keep seeing you – I believe you keep trying to tell me something. I think it might be important.'

'Oh yes, dear. It's very important. But it's time for my tea. You should come back tomorrow.'

Dom touches my back. 'Come on, Ella. Let it go. She's just a confused old woman. You're not going to get any sense out of her.'

I nod. Whoever this benign old lady is, she is not the monster of my hallucinations, and she can't help me. She doesn't remember an accident and she has no idea who I am. Although I'm still certain that she is somehow connected to my predicament, I know I am going to have to find the answers elsewhere. 'OK, thank you,' I say. 'I'll come back tomorrow then.'

'Don't mention it, dear,' she says, and I watch as she shuffles off down the high street.

21

Wrestling with an Octopus

I try hard not to let my knowledge that the old woman is flesh and blood after all, or the revelation that I have – or had – a boyfriend so secret that I wasn't aware of him myself, spoil my date with Will. I'm getting good at blocking out things that would send most people over the edge (although some might say that's because I double-backflipped off it many weeks ago). It helps that he takes me to the cinema to see a movie in 3D, a brainless action movie that's so noisy and so packed with special effects that it would be impossible to think about anything else, even if you wanted to. I also have to contend with the distraction of his wandering hands, which keep trying to find their way up under my top and down inside the waistband of my jeans. It is, as Deeta used to say – not about Will specifically, obviously – like wrestling with a human octopus. The movie has so many explosions and special effects that light up the screen and momentarily illuminate the room, I'm sure the poor woman sitting on the other side of me can tell exactly what's going on. She shuffles uncomfortably in her seat, staring straight ahead, keeping her 3D glasses on even in the non 3D bits, and shovelling handfuls of popcorn into her mouth until the credits roll and the lights come back up. When she leaves, she turns away from us and walks right to the other end of the row, even though we're sitting right by the aisle.

Will is oblivious to anyone else's discomfort; he just can't keep his hands off me. That's a fact, not a boast; I have no claim to being irresistible. When he isn't trying to navigate his way into my knickers in dark rooms or cars, he's trailing his arm around my shoulders while we walk, or concertinaing his fingers in-between mine, or leaning down to kiss my forehead. I'm not going to lie and say it's unpleasant, because it isn't, and I have nothing against public displays of affection (unless they involve people over thirty), but it's just a little too much. Then again, if I really am his first proper girlfriend, and this is all new to him, he's bound to be overexcited. It reminds me of how affectionate Billy used to be before every kiss or touch had a subtext, before I stopped trusting him.

Something else that reminds me of Billy – and also, unfortunately, of the main reason that I stopped trusting him – is the conversation I have with Will later that evening, soon after he's dropped me home. We are messaging each other from our beds, our words becoming more and more flirtatious, when he types: *Go on then, send me a picture of yourself. I'd really like to see you now.*

I feel a pang of something I can't quite explain or name: sadness, regret, hurt, annoyance, anxiety, all mixed up together. I'm not stupid; I know exactly what he means. But I'm not going there. *OK*, I type. *Hold on a minute.* I switch on my bedside light, shape my mouth into a huge, fake grin and take a cheesy selfie on my phone. It sends and I lie back, waiting for his predictable response.

That's gorgeous but it's not what I meant. You know it isn't. I want to see you. All of you. Not just your face.

No way.

Why not? I promise I won't show anyone. You don't even have to have your head in it, just your body.

Charming. So I could be anyone then? Just a body, that's all that matters to him. *No, sorry*, I type, but I'm not sorry. I actually feel angry now: with Will for asking, with Billy for doing what he did, with myself for allowing it to happen.

Why not? Don't you trust me?

And there it is: the million-pound question. I want to say, No, because you won't be able to help yourself. You'll want your mates to know you have it to make them jealous and to think you're such a big man, and then one of them will work on you, teasing you and wearing you down until you show it to him. After that, somebody will make a copy and it will get around somehow. Someone else will see it and then someone else, and someone else until in the end, everyone has seen it, and even those who didn't will know about it. Or maybe it won't happen exactly like that. Maybe we'll just have an argument, or break up, and you'll want to get your revenge. Either way, the picture won't be private any more. I won't be private any more. That's how these things go. I know; I remember. I'm not stupid enough to make the same mistake twice.

Of course I trust you, I type, great big coward that I am. *I'm just feeling shy.*

You're not shy! How about I send you one of me first?

Do if you want, but I'm still not sending one of me.

I'll delete it straight after. Promise.

No you won't, I think. Why are boys so obsessed with seeing, with looking at pictures? Why can't they just use their imaginations? Why do they have to use their eyes to get turned on?

Not now, Will. Please stop pressuring me.

I'm sorry, I didn't mean to upset you.

It's OK. Although it isn't.

And then he says something I'm not expecting at all, something that Billy didn't say once, not in all our years together. He says: *I'd never do anything to hurt you, Ella. We've got a special connection. I felt it the moment I met you.*

I don't know how to reply. I probably would have said the same thing myself, if you'd asked the old Ella, but now I'm sure it was just wishful thinking. I believe in chemistry, sure, but there's no such thing as a soulmate. There's just who you happen to meet at a particular time, in a particular place – the person you bump into depending on whether you turn left or right. Love is random. The romantic in me would like to think Will feels we have a connection because he can sense an echo from the other universe in which we are together. But the cynic in me knows that he's probably just talking bullshit because he wants me to send him a naked selfie.

I don't know how to reply. So I just type: *I know.*

22

Show Me the Mummy

I wait for Dom in the courtyard of the British Museum, under a roof made of up thousands of panes of triangular glass, which form a giant mosaic of the sky. I'm not entirely sure what I'm doing here; Will wouldn't be happy if he knew I was meeting another guy, and I've got college work I need to finish. Yet something – a mixture of curiosity and politeness, perhaps – makes me come. And now I'm here, I'm glad I did. Dom could not have known it when he suggested this place, but he really couldn't have picked anywhere more apt for me. The British Museum is like a Tardis: at the same time both ancient and modern, a portal to past worlds, other places and times. Turn in one direction and you're in ancient Egypt, turn another and you're in Greece or Rome. I like feeling that I'm a part of something bigger, that there have always been other worlds within this one.

As I see Dom approach, I realise with certainty and some relief that I don't fancy him at all. It seems hard to believe that the other me did. Surely it's more than just circumstance and shared experience that attracts us to people? I suppose that Dom might be someone you have to get to know really well before you fancy him, but I can't imagine it. Still, that's a good thing. I have a boyfriend. What I need right now are friends, and Dom strikes me as a good one, someone you can depend on, someone who'll protect you like a big brother. I will say this for him: he may not do it for me physically, but he's a hell of a lot more interesting than Will. He knows facts about all kinds of subjects: history and art and architecture and even fashion. He knows about the tools and the types of paint and precious metals that people used thousands of years ago. And the way he talks about these things to me suggests that the other me knew about them too.

'So go on then, show me di mummy,' I joke. You've got to have seen this old Tom Cruise movie called *Jerry Maguire* to get it, but I figure that Dom has. 'That's why we're here, isn't it?'

He laughs. 'You're the one who wanted to see the mummies – I've seen them loads of times. I'll take you now – they're upstairs.'

Although I still can't conceive of why the other me was so desperate to see dead people swaddled in bandages, once we walk into the rooms where the mummies are kept I have to acknowledge that they are fascinating. We're not just looking at statues; these are real people, who died thousands of years ago, ancient Egyptians no less, the people who built the pyramids and who might have known Cleopatra! And yet here they are: two thousand miles away, in glass cases in a room in Bloomsbury, central London, being gawped at by twenty-first-century tourists, who are taking photos on their smartphones. When they thought about the afterlife, I'm sure these Egyptians never imagined that it would mean being entombed in a London museum for all eternity.

Just like me, these poor people really have ended up in some sort of parallel universe.

'I know how they must feel,' I say to Dom, vocalising my thoughts. 'If dead people could feel, that is.'

'What did you say?'

'I said I can relate to them, because they're sort of trapped in a parallel universe, a bit like me.'

He starts laughing. 'Good one. You think you're trapped in a parallel universe. So is Doctor Who going to turn up wearing a fez in a second?'

I've got to admit it does sound a bit ridiculous, said out loud. 'No, I'm deadly serious. That's what I think has happened to me. It makes perfect sense – it's really the only thing that does.'

'If I didn't know you, Ella, I'd say you were on something.'

This irritates me, even though it's not his fault. He doesn't really know me; that's the point. He thinks he does, but he knows another Ella. 'It's not down to anything chemical. It's physics. I've discussed it with Dan . . . Mr Perry, my tutor. In fact, it's his theory.'

'And Mr Perry says you've jumped universes? Wow. I know I left college a few years ago but I think I missed that lesson. That and the one about unicorns.'

I choose to ignore his sarcasm. 'Yes. My consciousness has. We're just not sure why yet. It all makes perfect sense when he explains it. Multiverses are what he's doing his thesis on – for his PhD.'

'Come off it. You're acting like he's Einstein, but he's just a student and what he's planting in your head is a load of bollocks. I don't know what he's getting out of it, but it's not normal.'

I wish I hadn't told him now. 'You sound . . .' I want to say 'jealous' but that would be mean in the circumstances. 'Paranoid.'

'No, I'm just being protective. I'm a guy and I know what guys are like. He obviously wants something from you. You're vulnerable and he's messing with your head.'

'My head is already messed up.'

'Yeah, exactly. So he shouldn't be making it worse.'

'OK then, if you're so sure his theory is bollocks, what do *you* think has happened to me?'

He shrugs. 'Amnesia, like they say. Maybe depression. I dunno. Something medical. Definitely not anything sci-fi.'

I pout at him. 'Think whatever you like, but I'm not sick. And one day I'll be able to prove it.'

'Course you will,' he says. 'Listen, why don't we take a break and go get a coffee? Lighten the mood a bit?'

The coffee doesn't stop me feeling sulky. I hate that the first – and only – person I've trusted with my situation is so disbelieving, and that he's questioned Daniel's motives when Daniel is on my side and he's the only one who hasn't treated me like I'm going crazy. Now I feel stupid and confused again, and very alone. When I tell Dom I'm going to go home because I have things to do, he looks disappointed, like he's blown a date, even though I know he never had a chance in the first place.

Soon after I arrive home, I receive a text from Rachel. *Call me ASAP*, it reads. *We need to talk*. The brevity and urgency of her message makes me wonder what might have happened. The lack of a kiss – or any warmth or affection – makes me nervous too, because it suggests that I'm in big trouble. The problem is, I have no idea what I might have done or, quite possibly, what I might have forgotten to do. Swallowing hard, I call her back. She picks up instantly.

'Hey, Rachel,' I say brightly, in an attempt to ward off any disapproval. 'I just got your text. Everything OK?'

'Hello, Ella.' I've never heard Rachel sound so cold.

'What's up?'

She sighs. 'Stuff. I'm . . . really disappointed in you.'

This is a sentence that I've heard many times: from my parents, from teachers, from Billy when I didn't live up to his expectations of how I should dress or behave. Yet I don't think it's something people say to the other Ella very often. Oh God. I really don't need this right now. 'Why? What have I done?'

She takes a deep breath, as if she's about to launch into a long list of my failings. 'Well, for starters, I didn't think you were the type of girl who dumped her mates for a boy.'

'Oh.' I'm not sure what to say to that. The thing is, to my shame, I kind of am. I was always cancelling on my friends to be with Billy. Deeta often did it to me too. Neither of us liked it but it was accepted as something that sometimes couldn't be helped, mainly because boys are so disorganised, and spontaneity is a good thing. 'I'm sorry. I didn't think anything much was happening last night. I didn't think you'd mind my not being there.'

'Yeah? Well, we did. Jen and I were looking forward to having a girlie night with you, but as soon as some boy asks you out you just drop us, like you don't give a toss.'

'It wasn't like that,' I say. Except it was, really, wasn't it? 'Look, I'm sorry. It won't happen again. OK? It was only our second date and I wasn't expecting him to ask me out again so soon. It's going well. You've both got to meet him.'

'Meet who?'

'Will, obviously.' I laugh. 'Who else?'

'I don't know, Ella. You keep talking about your new boyfriend Will, but that's not who I saw you with yesterday, is it?'

'What are you talking about?'

'Don't play dumb, Ella. I know you've made up all that stuff about seeing Will. I thought it was weird how you'd never even mentioned him before a few weeks ago and then you suddenly start "dating" him. But I took your word for it until yesterday, until I caught you red-handed! I was on the high street doing some shopping and I thought, Ooh, it's about the time Ella finishes work, I'll pop in and say hi. But then I looked through the window, and there you are with Dom – sitting at a table, having a cosy chat. Jen's Dom, Ella. You know how upset she is about him. How could you?'

I giggle, relieved. She actually thinks I've invented a fantasy relationship with Will to mask a real one with Dom. What a bizarre notion. 'Don't be silly. You've got it all wrong; I am going out with Will, and Dom is just a mate. In fact, I'd completely forgotten who he was.'

And then my relief evaporates because I realise that she's half right: in this universe I have secretly been seeing Dom. Even though *I'm* not lying, the Ella she knows is.

'OK, then. Swear on your life that you're not seeing Dom.'

Swear on my life? On which life? I'm not generally superstitious, but I do take swearing on my life about anything as a solemn oath. If I agree to do it, will something terrible happen to me, to the new Ella, or to both of us? Will it make the universes crash into each other and explode? 'Don't be silly, Rachel. Just take my word for it. Maybe it was stupid of me to meet Dom and not tell you about it, but he's not my boyfriend.'

'I don't know if I believe you.'

'You're not going to tell Jen about this, are you?' I'm guessing she hasn't already done so, hence this conversation. She's sounding me out first.

'I don't know. I don't like keeping stuff from her.'

'I know. But what's the point? It would only hurt her.'

'So now you care about hurting her. If you've been lying, she deserves to know. I mean, you even encouraged her to go for it with him! And all the time you knew he was going to reject her because he was with you. That's sick!'

'Come on! It wasn't like that. I'd never do that.'

'I'd like to believe you but I'm not sure I can. You've been acting so weirdly lately.'

'You know why that is.'

202

'No, it's more than that. You've changed: the way you act, the way you think, the way you react to things. Sometimes I think I don't know who you are any more.'

Wow. There it is: the truth at last. I'm not the Ella she knows, the studious, sweet, hospice-volunteering, virginal, goody two-shoes. I'm someone else altogether – someone, it's pretty clear, who she doesn't even like very much. Hearing it hurts a lot more than I might have predicted it would, for, even though Rachel wouldn't be my number one choice of best friend, I do like her and I want her to like me back.

I don't say anything in response; what can I say? Somehow, I don't think she'd react well to an explanation that involves parallel worlds and multiple versions of me. It's funny how what made so much sense when Daniel explained it, just a couple of days ago, now sounds like a fantastical excuse for being a rubbish friend. And for being a rubbish person too.

'I should go,' says Rachel eventually. 'Call me when you feel like being honest with me.' She puts the phone down without saying goodbye and I feel like I've lost something important, even though I didn't really care about it that much when I had it.

I lie on my bed feeling sorry for myself for a while, wondering how I've managed to end up so isolated, when I've always had lots of friends. There's been an email in my inbox for a few days from the local arthouse cinema, offering tickets for a one-off showing of a restored Louise Brooks film called *Pandora's Box*. It's a tragedy about a woman called Lulu who is beautiful and wild and doesn't live by anybody else's rules. It seems like fate that they're showing it now;

her films are hardly ever on. I've been mulling over buying a couple of tickets and asking if anyone would like to come with me. But there's absolutely no point asking Will, who has no interest in art-house movies and will just see it as a good excuse to feel me up in the dark. Even if Rachel were speaking to me, I know it's not her or Jen's thing either. We were talking about the cinema once, and Jen said straight out, 'I won't watch anything in black and white,' as if it would make her eyes bleed. The only person who might want to come with me is Dom, but after my conversation with Rachel, asking him seems like a foolish notion. Plus, I don't think it would be sensible to see too much of him because it could give him the wrong idea. I should probably just go alone . . . and yet I keep thinking that perhaps this is the very excuse I need to reconnect with Deeta.

It's worth one last shot, isn't it? In another universe, at our sixteenth birthday party (we shared parties, even though our birthdays are months apart) we managed to get hold of an old projector and we projected YouTube clips from the film on to a huge white sheet, which we'd hung from the ceiling, as a backdrop. We were so pleased with ourselves.

I input the number I know so well into my phone and type: *Hi, it's Ella from college here. I know you don't really know me, but a little bird told me you like Louise Brooks films too, and they're showing* Pandora's Box *at the Curzon. Would you like to come with me?*

The words don't seem right, but none that I can think of do. So I press send and let the message fly away, and pray that this time, the Deeta in this universe will give me a chance.

Later, when I finally go to bed, I can't sleep again. When at last I drop off, I dream of mummies lying in gilded coffins, enclosed in glass sarcophagi. I dream of myself as a mummy: swaddled, trapped, unable to move, as a shrill beeping sound grows in intensity all around me. Out of the corner of my eye, I can see another mummy lying next to me, her coffin painted with the old woman's face. Her expression is angry, contorted and I want to flee, but I can't.

Then everything turns to black and white, and I am Louise Brooks, wordless and silently screaming, as the old woman rises from her coffin and looms above me.

23

Rejection

Deeta doesn't reply to my text, but I have my answer just a few days later, when I bump into her in the locker room at college. For once, we are both alone and so I take the opportunity to go over and say hello. She has her back to me, as she's putting something away in her locker, and I loiter behind her for a minute, hoping she'll turn to face me. She doesn't. She's wearing tracksuit bottoms and a red-and-white stripy cardigan. I still can't get used to seeing her in clothes I don't recognise, or didn't buy with her; I have to hold myself back from commenting 'New dress?' or 'Nice jeans'.

'Hey,' I say at last, as casually as I can. 'How's it going?' I feel nervous, the way you do after you've had an argument with someone and haven't spoken for a while, and now hope that they've forgiven you – except we've had no argument, because that requires a prior relationship.

She stops what she's doing and swings round, her eyes wide. 'God! You scared me!'

I don't think that can be true; I'm sure she must have sensed somebody was there, but then Deeta always did like to be dramatic. Still, this is a time to humour her. 'Sorry, didn't mean to.'

She turns away from me again and busies herself inside her locker. 'So what do you want?'

'Um . . . I just wondered if you'd got my text about *Pandora*.'

'Who?'

'The film: *Pandora's Box*. You know, "Lulu". Like I said in the text, I heard you liked it too and I, er, have a spare ticket so I thought you might want it.'

She looks over her shoulder. 'Oh, that. Sorry, but why the hell would I want it? I'm not being rude or anything, but I don't even know you.'

'I know you think that but . . . I thought, well, we've got something in common and we're in the same year and . . . I don't know.' I'm aware that I sound pathetic. 'Anyway. If you want it, it's yours.'

She turns back round, stands up straight and unexpectedly moves towards me, coming up so close to my face that I can smell a trace of something sweet on her breath. 'Listen. It's Ella, right?' I nod. 'Look, I don't know what is going on with you, but I've heard you're not quite right in the head, so I'm going to spell this out to you nice and clearly.' She points her finger at me. It's not gnarled like the old woman's, but it feels just as threatening. 'We don't know each other, we are not friends and we're not going to be friends. End of. I've got all the friends I need and I don't get your sudden interest in me. I also don't get why you think I'd want to go to the cinema with you or why you presume I'd be desperate to see some ancient, silent movie that I saw once and frankly didn't rate all that much, but I don't. OK? So please leave me alone. Stop staring at me. Stop following me. Stop texting me. Because if you don't I will report you for stalking me, you freak. All right?' Shocked, I nod again and she takes a step back from me. 'Now piss off.'

Tears begin to prick at the back of my eyes as I walk away. It's one thing not being remembered, but quite another being so roundly rejected. I always knew that Deeta had it in her to be mean, and yet in all our years of friendship she'd never focused that meanness on me; I naively thought I was immune. I had forgotten that Deeta only does things when she wants, on her terms and now that I'm not on her radar any more, I have nothing to offer her. What niggles me most is that I can't understand why she doesn't seem to like me, why she has no interest in me. I guess I'd hoped that, as with Will, I could somehow get through to her and start up our relationship again. Show her what you're about, I thought, and she'll know that you're meant to be best friends; she'll sense it.

I am also mystified as to why she doesn't like *Pandora's Box*, the film that we bonded over. Am I misremembering our past? Was it, in fact, me who introduced her to Louise Brooks, and not the other way around? And if that's the case, what else might I be remembering wrongly? Whatever the truth, how stupid I was to try to buy her friendship with cinema tickets, how foolish and how desperate. I cringe at myself, digging my nails into my palms and squeezing my eyes shut.

The hurt hangs over me for days. I play back my friendship with Deeta over and over in my mind, remembering all the things I think we shared, the laughs we had together. It doesn't seem possible that we became best friends only because I happened to be in the right place at the right time, that I could have been anyone. But if that is the case, then perhaps there is a way to fix it.

At my next session with Daniel I ask if it's feasible for me to climb into some kind of time machine, like the ones I've seen in movies, and go back to the night of the party, so that I can change my decision, and choose to attend. Surely, if I make certain that I have met Deeta in this universe, in the same way that I did in the other, when I arrive back in the present we will be best mates again.

Daniel shakes his head. He tells me that although it is theoretically possible, it can't be done, and the consequences would be disastrous. 'There's no such thing as a time machine,' he says. 'If it were possible, don't you think we'd be meeting time tourists all the time, people who've come from the future or the past? I've never met one. Have you?'

'Maybe they just don't tell anybody they're time travellers,' I suggest. 'Like me, not going round telling everyone that I'm trapped in the wrong universe. Maybe they're scared people will think they're crazy.'

He nods. 'Perhaps. Ella, you haven't told anyone else about our conversations, have you?'

I cast my eyes downwards. I'm a terrible liar, always have been. 'Only one person, a friend. Not anyone from college. I didn't say much.'

Daniel looks anxious. 'And this friend, what did they say?'

'Not a lot. They didn't believe the parallel-universe stuff, so I dropped it.'

'Tell me exactly what they said, Ella. I need to know.'

'Honestly?' I giggle, nervously. 'All right, then. They think I'm bonkers and you're talking bollocks, and that I shouldn't listen to you. They even said that you're trying to mess with my head. As if, huh? I mean, what could you possibly be getting out of it?'

I grin at him, so he knows that's not what I think, and that I'm on his side, but he's not smiling back. In fact, he looks so quietly angry that he's transformed into one of those black holes that he talks about – sucking all the energy in the room into himself until he's about to implode with rage. His face is red from forehead to chin, his jaw clenched and his eyes wildly unfocused.

'Do you think this is a joke?' he says. He doesn't bellow at me – it would be less scary if he did. His voice is quiet and tight and perfectly controlled. 'Do you think I'm just playing at this? If I wanted, if you had the capability and the knowledge and the insight to be able to understand them, I could show you academic books and notebooks full of equations and calculations and theories that prove what I am saying. We may talk about gold shoes here, Ella, but I assure you that that is purely for your benefit. There are, dare I say it, no gold shoes in the annals of physics. This is my life's work and the life's work of other scientists who have come before me.

'Because of your personal situation I have let you have access to knowledge that is not yet understood enough or developed enough to be revealed publicly. It is not to be ridiculed. Do you understand?' He pauses to clear his throat. 'If you don't take it seriously, if I can't trust you not to talk about it to your friends, who cannot be relied upon to keep it to themselves and who aren't knowledgeable enough to understand it, then I might have to suggest that someone else tutors you.'

'Oh,' I manage to squeak out, aware that I am holding myself so still, so tense, that I have begun to shake. Until now, until I was faced with losing him, I was not aware how much I needed Daniel and his insights. The thought of being sent out into the darkness, to deal with the confusion of my life alone again, petrifies me. It's only since I started our sessions that I've been able to think straight at all. 'I'm sorry. I didn't mean to blab. I do take what you say to me seriously. And I don't want another tutor. You're the only person who understands what's happening to me. Please don't stop helping me; I don't know what I'd do if you did.'

He nods slowly, staring into my eyes as if he's trying to read my thoughts. I think, perhaps, that he can read my thoughts. 'I will continue to help you on condition that you don't question my motives again. And that you never tell anyone the content of what we discuss. This is between us and us alone. Is that agreed?'

'Yes. Agreed. Of course, Daniel. I promise. I won't let you down.'

I've never meant anything more in my life. I mustn't let him down. I can't let him down. There's still so much I need to figure out.

24

An Accidental Killer

Daniel and I meet up frequently over the next few weeks, both at my allotted tutorial times and, more and more often, on other days too. I am probably spending more time with him than I am with any of my friends, apart from Will (and he doesn't really count as a friend). Although Rachel has forgiven me for meeting Dom and, surprisingly, didn't tell Jen about it in the end, I have sensed an even greater and widening distance between the three of us, one that I haven't tried to repair. We just go through the motions, like we're on autopilot. As for Dom, I've only seen him once, briefly, since our British Museum trip. I know that if I spend too much time talking to him, I'll end up saying something I shouldn't about Daniel.

My parents still think I'm seeing the counsellor, but I haven't been back since my first session. I meet Daniel when I should be having my appointments with her. As I appear more stable, they assume that the sessions are working, and don't ask too many questions. It helps that they're barely speaking to one another. If one of them does happen to ask anything, I fudge my answers; counselling is supposed to be confidential, isn't it? I guess they'll find out I'm not going eventually.

Daniel and I dedicate very little time to the college syllabus any more. Instead, we usually get straight to talking about me and my parallel existence, which suits me. I've stopped caring about what grades I get, or whether I can switch courses. Why does it matter, when I'm not planning to stick around here for much longer? The fact is, the more lonely I feel in this world, the more desperate I become to find a way to return to my original universe. Daniel says he thinks he can help me to do that, but first he needs to know every tiny detail about me and about my life as the other Ella. 'Write it down,' he says. 'Write it all down. Everything you have experienced, everything you remember, however insignificant it seems, however irrelevant to your situation you think it may be. Let me study it.'

That's how I come to tell him about my déjà vu experience in the scanning machine and the beeps I sometimes hear in my sleep, and about the old woman, who is at once both real and a hallucination. The more I talk about her, the more excited Daniel becomes.

'I don't think you have been hallucinating,' he says. 'Have you ever thought that she might exist both as a real person and as a projected image of that person?'

'You mean like a ghost?'

'Yes, I suppose I do. In fact, some say that what people call "ghosts" are really glimpses of people in other universes.

213

Given your apparent transfer of consciousness, it is possible that at the times you believe you are hallucinating the old woman, you are actually getting a glimpse of her from your other universe.'

This makes a weird kind of sense to me. The old woman does present like something supernatural, a ghost or a spectre. 'But why would she haunt me? And why does she appear so angry and threatening in that universe, when she's so frail and clueless here?'

He takes a deep breath. 'I have a theory about that too. I think, perhaps, that you did hit her with your car in the other universe – an accident you can't remember. You could have severely injured or, more likely, even have killed her there. Maybe that is why your near miss in this universe was enough of a jolt to make your consciousness transfer across. Some things, it seems clear, are destined to happen in every universe. It's possible that running over the old lady is one them.'

I suddenly feel cold inside, even though I'm wearing a chunky sweater. 'You think that I killed her? You think I killed someone?' I shake my head. No, no, no. It's too much to take in.

'Not intentionally. But yes. You may well have done so accidentally. Or perhaps you were just the passenger in the car that killed her. You say that on one occasion when the old woman "appeared" to you and was particularly frightening, Will was driving, although he didn't see her. Maybe that's because Billy hit her in your original universe, and you were with him in the car.'

'I don't know. How can I know? Everything's maybe or perhaps. How can I find out for certain?'

'The proof lies in the other universe, I'm afraid. If I am right, then if you jumped back across you would find evidence there.'

'So you're saying that if I go back to my other life, the old lady will be dead?'

He nods. 'It seems likely.'

I'm on the brink of tears now. 'Then me going back means killing her? But if I stay here, she's alive. So if I go back I'll actually be murdering her! Oh God!'

He smiles at me, which seems a weird reaction. 'No, Ella, because there she is already dead. Here she will still be alive, wandering happily up and down the high street with her shopping trolley, just as you describe her. Going back – or more accurately, across – won't change anything here.'

'But where will I find myself when I get there? I mean, if I was in a car that killed someone, maybe I'll go back and discover I got arrested and I'm in prison or some young offenders' place. Or Billy is. Or worse, what if I'm dead?'

'I've told you: you can't be dead there, Ella, because we have established that your consciousness has come across to your body here. If original Ella were dead, her consciousness would also be dead.'

There's something that still doesn't make sense to me. 'The last thing I remember is going to a party with Billy, and hanging out with Deeta. I don't remember an accident. How can that be?'

'It's likely that your mind has blanked out the accident, owing to its traumatic nature. The last thing you remember in your original universe is not the last thing that happened there – clearly, because you are still continuing to exist there. But the accident you had here, in the car with your father, must have been the trigger to bring your consciousness across, even if you didn't immediately become aware of it. The concussion that you suffered following your brief moment of unconsciousness allowed it to happen. Are you following me?'

I nod. 'I think so. Go on.'

'So why, we ask ourselves, has this happened? And why at this juncture? And, more to the point, how on earth are you managing to exist back there without your consciousness, if it is here now, in this body? To explain this, I have another theory . . .' He lets his words dangle enticingly, knowing that I am already desperate to hear his explanation.

I'm holding my breath. 'Yes, go on, please.'

'I believe that in your original universe, as a result of the accident that may have killed the old woman, you were also injured – so seriously, in fact, that you died for a millisecond and at that moment your consciousness was released. You ended up in a coma and you remain in hospital there, in a deep state of unconsciousness. The bleeps of machinery you think you hear sometimes when you are falling asleep or waking up are the hospital monitors, which are keeping you alive. The reason that you felt you had been in a scanning machine before was not due to déjà vu. It was because you have – not here, but in the other universe. And when you sense you are being held down, it is because there, in your comatose state, you are hooked up to machines and drips, with a mask over your face, unable to move or breathe for yourself. These are not dreams, Ella, they are fragments of awareness leaking through the chasm between the universes.'

'Oh God.' I don't seem to be able to control my legs; they're all weak and shaky. 'So if I go back, I'll be in a coma?' It doesn't seem like much of a choice: stay here and be miserable and lonely and a misfit, or go back there and be a vegetable.

'No, Ella. I think the only reason you haven't woken from your coma is because your consciousness is here, in this universe. It's logical: if you have no consciousness, you must surely remain unconscious. But were you to go back, your consciousness would return, and so you would instantaneously come out of the coma and awaken.'

Now I'm excited. 'So if I go back, I'll actually be saving myself twice? I'll have my proper life back and I'll be rescuing myself from a coma.'

'Yes,' he says. 'You've got it.'

'And if I don't go back?' I already know this isn't an option for me, but I need to know the answer.

'It's possible that at some point your original consciousness from this universe – which is being blocked out or suppressed by your other consciousness at present – will find its way to the surface, or be triggered to return by something, and then you will forget that you ever had another life and just carry on living here as before.'

'That wouldn't be so bad,' I say. 'Would it? Although I've buggered everything up now with my friends and with college.'

'No, it wouldn't be so bad. But that might not happen, and I'm afraid that the alternative . . . the alternative is far worse. You see, what I fear most for you is that your coma goes on for too long – for months and months – and the doctors eventually decide that you are unlikely ever to recover. It is possible that they may advise your parents to switch you off.'

'Switch me off? And what happens if they do?'

'You'll die in the other universe. And that means you'd never be able to go back across. Your consciousness would be extinguished, and that could have serious implications; we cannot predict what might happen. You could be in a vegetative state here too. There is no way to guarantee that your other consciousness will take over. It may have been utterly squashed, or destroyed.'

'So I've got to go back then, haven't I?! There's no choice. And the sooner the better! Tell me, please, how do I go back?' It's a question I've asked several times, but he never seems to want to give me a direct answer.

'I still don't think you're ready to know,' he says. 'There is more I need to share with you first, and you've already got a lot to take in and digest today.'

At our next session, he takes a blue paper folder from his briefcase and hands it to me. It's covered in scribbles, half-finished equations and scientific doodles that make no sense to me. When I doodle, it's always faces and eyes and the things I notice around me. Daniel doodles only numbers and symbols. 'Here, open it,' he says. Inside, there is a bundle of papers. 'Take these and have a look through. They are proof that while you are unusual, you are not alone, not the only one. These people felt the same as you: that they were trapped in an alternate version of their lives, that they'd slipped into another universe.'

I carry the papers back to my desk and start reading through them, as quickly as I can, barely breathing as I do so. The bundle includes printouts of blog posts, letters and emails, some of which are directly addressed to Daniel, and they recount the experiences of both men and women of varying ages, from all around the country. There's nobody as young as me, and nobody who lives locally. But what they say sounds very familiar: 'I woke up and it was like I was living another life'; 'I'm not me any more. I look like me but everything else has changed'; 'This man says he's my husband but I don't know him at all. I'm supposed to be married to someone else.' Their stories become increasingly desperate: 'Nobody believes me. They think I'm losing it'; 'Help me, please. I can't carry on like this'; 'My wife says she's going to get me sectioned'; 'I don't want to live here any more. I want to go back to my own life.' Any one of these people could be me. I'm not sure if I feel happy or relieved or scared.

'Hey, slow down,' says Daniel. 'You don't have to read them all now. You can take them home with you tonight – as long as you don't show anyone or leave them around anywhere. I'll need them back at our next session.'

'Thank you, of course.' I catch my breath. 'I didn't know you'd met people like me before, Daniel.'

'Oh yes,' he says. 'I came across them all during my research, over the past few years. It's partly why I was so keen to tutor you. There are almost certainly others: these are just the ones I know of, the ones who talked openly about their experiences. I have corresponded with them all and can verify their stories.'

I rewind what he just said to me. He was so keen to tutor me? I assumed the college had decided he was the best person; I didn't realise he'd engineered our meetings. Now I can't remember when it was that I first told him what I felt had happened to me. Was it when our sessions started, or could he just tell from meeting me, when I was upset? Did he sense something in me, something that he'd seen in the others? I suppose it doesn't really matter now.

'So can I talk to them? It would be great to meet someone else like me.'

He sighs. 'I was hoping you wouldn't ask that of me, Ella. I'm afraid that won't be possible.'

'Why not? I wouldn't – won't – tell anyone. It would be completely secret. And it would help me so much. Like, you have no idea how much.'

'I'm sorry, but it's not going to happen.'

'Don't you trust me, Daniel? I haven't mentioned what we talk about to anyone else, not since you told me off about it. And these people, you could ask them first if it's OK for me to contact them, or even just give them my email and tell them to get in touch with me. Or just one of them. I don't need to speak to all of them . . .'

'Of course I trust you, Ella. That's not the reason I'm saying no. Believe me, I am not being obstructive. The truth is, I would dearly like to speak to them myself, if only I could.'

He pauses, and his voice drops almost to a whisper. 'I didn't want to tell you this yet, because I don't think you're ready to hear it. The reason you can't speak to any of them is because they are all dead.'

25

The Only One Left Alive

I think somebody just kicked me in the stomach. Kicked me in the stomach and then left their foot inside me. Dead? All of them? I can't have heard right. 'That can't be true. How?'

Daniel doesn't look me in the eye. 'I'm not really sure of the details.'

He's obviously being evasive, but why? For a split second I wonder if they all had some sort of fatal disease – an infection or a brain tumour that causes delusional thoughts and hallucinations – and he doesn't want to have to tell me that I have it too. But that wouldn't tally with anything else he's said to me over the past weeks, and I've had scans and tests that show I'm not ill. Could he simply be lying? Perhaps they're not dead at all; he just doesn't want me to contact them. 'I don't believe you. Tell me, Daniel. Please.'

'It won't help you to know this now. We'll talk about it more next time, I promise, but not now. We've gone way over schedule, and they'll be locking up the college soon. I'm running late. It's time to go.'

He starts to put his notes away in his bag and to reach for his overcoat, which hangs messily over the back of his chair, one sleeve trailing on the dusty ground. I stand still for a moment, just watching him, and then I make for the back of the room and position myself in front of the door, arms spread, feet firmly together. There is no way he is going to leave this room without telling me what I need to know. No way. By now he has his coat on and he is starting to walk towards me, a puzzled expression on his face. 'What are you doing, Ella? Session's over – we're leaving now. Go and get your stuff together and get your coat. There's a good girl.'

I've said it before: I don't like being patronised. His attitude makes me more determined than ever. I shake my head at him and lean against the door, so that all my weight is on it, the handle poking into the small of my back. If he is going to open it, he'll have to reach around me and shove me out of the way. I don't think he's going to do that. Not Daniel. 'No!' I shout. 'Not until you tell me.'

'Oh for goodness' sake, Ella, grow up and move away from the door. It's for your own good that I'm not telling you. It's not something to be rushed. Now, I've got to be somewhere and I'm in a hurry. Please move away from the door.'

'No,' I repeat. 'Not until you tell me. I'm sick of not knowing things that are important.'

He comes up to me, really close, so close that I am suddenly afraid. I remember what he was like when he was really

223

angry, when he told me off about talking to Dom; he had simmered like an underground volcano. Now I'm scared of what he might do to me. He places his hands tightly on my shoulders and I hold my breath, certain that he's about to pull me or push me or shake me, or hurt me in some way. But he doesn't. Instead, he looks into my eyes and says gently, 'Move away from the door, Ella, and I promise I will tell you the truth.' He doesn't look angry, he's virtually smiling. Or is it smirking?

I find myself doing as he says, almost without willing it, my legs stepping aside so that he is free to open the door. He reaches out to grab the door handle, and shakes his head. 'You kept your end of the bargain, so I will keep mine now and tell you. But, believe me, you aren't going to thank me for it.' He opens the door, as if ready to make his escape, and sighs. 'They are all dead, Ella, because they killed themselves. Each of them chose to take his or her own life. Now you know.'

With that, he shakes his head again, pushes the door wider and walks into the corridor. And I am left melted, like the Wicked Witch of the West, nothing remaining of me but a crumpled heap of rags on the floor.

I'm not sure how I get home; I don't remember the journey. But once I am back in my bedroom all I can think about is discovering as much as I can about what happened to these people, and why. Using the sheets that Daniel has given me as a reference, I Google each of them in turn, finding local newspaper reports and Facebook tribute pages. Maureen Fellows, fifty-nine, who had a kindly face

224

and wispy blonde hair, was found dead at her home in Ipswich. She had taken an overdose and left a note saying that she believed she was trapped in the wrong universe. The inquest said the 'balance of her mind was disturbed'. John O'Reilly, thirty-four, was found hanged in the woods near his home. He had recently lost his job and was being treated for depression and alcoholism. Lisa Cromwell, twenty-one, the one who was nearest my age, disappeared on Christmas Eve. Her car was found abandoned by the cliffs at Beachy Head, but her body has never been found. Her friends at university reported that in the weeks leading up to her disappearance she seemed withdrawn and not her usual bubbly self. Michael Turner, forty-three, hanged himself at his home in Manchester. He'd pretended to go to work, sat in McDonald's for a few hours without buying anything, and then returned home to take his life. His wife found him when she came back that evening. Sonia Patel, twenty-nine, took an overdose. She was supposed to be getting married just one month later.

The last one is the most chilling of all: Kerry Lawton, thirty-seven, died in a fire at her home, which also killed her partner and seven-month-old baby. It is believed to have been started deliberately.

All dead and in horrible ways.

And now I'm the only one left.

I shiver, wrapping my cardigan more tightly around me. Daniel was right. Again. Learning this information has not helped me. Now that I know it, I wish I could un-know it. I wish I could scrub it out of my brain, together with this stupid consciousness. Acid rises into my throat and I know I'm going to be sick, just like I was the first morning I woke up and found myself in the wrong world. This time, I make it to the toilet in time. After I've flushed, I stand there aimlessly for a few minutes, unsure what to do with myself. I need to talk to someone to stop this terrible knowledge boring a hole through my brain, but there's nobody I can tell, and even if there were, there's nobody who would understand why I am so affected by the suicides of half a dozen strangers. There's only Daniel.

He gave me his number once, for emergencies. I think this counts as one of those.

I text him, with no clue what to say, or even if he'll reply. Perhaps he wants me to suffer for holding him hostage and forcing the truth out of him. In the end, I settle on: *Daniel, I'm sorry for earlier. I'm not coping and I need to talk to you urgently. Can we meet?*

He doesn't reply immediately, and there's no way of knowing if he just hasn't seen my message or is punishing me. I sit on my bed, staring down at my phone until, to my immeasurable relief, he answers: *OK. But I can't be seen with you alone in public. Come to my flat – I'll text you my address in a second. Then memorise it, delete my messages and tell no one that you're coming.*

He doesn't live far from my house, in a street that I've never been down, near the tube station. I tell my parents I'm popping out to meet Rachel and then march round to his flat as quickly as I can. Halfway there, it occurs to me that I might be doing something dangerous. Nobody knows where I'm going, and what I've learned tonight has painted Daniel in a sinister light. Could he have had something to with all the suicides? Maybe they weren't suicides at all, just meant to look like that. Might I not be safe alone with him? But that's ridiculous; Daniel is not some maniac serial killer, going around the country murdering people and then staging suicides. He even told me that he wished the others were alive too, so he could talk to them.

So why are they all dead? Is it because they couldn't cope any more, because they had discovered there was no way back to their real lives? Is that the real horror that he's been avoiding telling me?

I arrive at his front door, both hot with sweat and cold with fear, out of breath and shivering. I'm surprised to find he lives above a kebab shop, although I'm not sure why, or what I expected. He lets me in via an intercom and tells me to walk up two flights of stairs. My legs feel tired and heavy, like they're dragging me back.

He's waiting for me at the top. 'Come in,' he says, holding open his front door and beckoning me inside. 'You didn't tell anyone you were coming, did you?'

'No,' I assure him, catching my breath. I look around me, taking in the fact that Daniel lives in just one room, a sparse bedsit with a bed, a tiny kitchen area, a desk, chest of drawers and a few bookshelves. There's a rug thrown over the window as a makeshift curtain and a picture of a telescope above his bed. What few clothes he has are hung from a hook on the door. I guess the toilet and bathroom must be outside in the hall somewhere. This is exactly the sort of place where a serial killer could murder someone. I wonder if there are any neighbours around to hear the screams.

'Take a seat,' he says, pointing to his bed. He must notice my reticence because he adds, 'Don't worry, I'll sit on the floor over here. As you can see, this isn't really a place meant for entertaining.'

I nod and try to smile. 'Thanks,' I say, and I perch on the corner of the bed. 'I'm sorry to come round like this. I didn't know what else to do.'

'I'm not going to say "I told you so", although it would be merited. Now do you see why you need me, Ella? Why you can't do this on your own? I'm guessing you have done some more research since we spoke earlier, and learned all the gruesome details.'

I nod again. 'It freaked me out, reading what happened to them all. I don't understand why. I'm scared, Daniel. I don't want to die.'

'They're not really dead,' he says. 'At least, they're only dead in this world.'

'What do you mean?'

'Remember I told you that it's possible to be alive in one universe and dead in another? They are dead here, but alive in the universe where they feel they should be. They haven't died, so much as gone back home.'

'How do you know that's true?'

'I don't. I have no proof. That's the tragedy; I can only theorise.'

228

'So are you saying they didn't kill themselves because they'd had enough and couldn't hack the way they were feeling any more, but they actually did it to jump universes?'

He nods. 'Exactly. That is how one jumps across – the information I've been avoiding telling you.'

'But what about their friends and families here? What about that woman, Kerry, who killed her husband and baby too?'

'A terrible accident, I believe. They weren't meant to be there.'

'Weren't meant? How do you know? Did she tell you what she was planning?'

Or worse, the thought strikes me, did Daniel tell her what to do? Horrified, I propel myself up from the bed. 'Did you help them plan their deaths, Daniel, to prove your theory?'

'Calm down, and stop putting two and two together and making five. What sort of Machiavellian monster do you take me for? I didn't help anyone plan anything, or tell anyone they had to take their own life. I simply explained my theory to people who desperately needed help, and each of them made an independent decision.'

I sit down again, not because I want to, but because my knees are beginning to buckle. 'Do you want me to kill myself too, Daniel?'

'Of course not,' he says. 'I don't want that. But, as I was planning to explain to you when I felt you were ready, it is the only way. You will come to see that. Surely you didn't think you'd just be able to click your sparkly heels three times and wish you were home?'

I don't know what I thought, but it wasn't this. 'You can't promise me that it's going to work, though, can you? You can't promise that I'll wake up back in my old body, in my old life? Because as you just said, you can't prove anything!'

I start to sob with frustration and self-pity, which makes me cry all the more because the last thing I want is for Daniel to see me losing it. I rub my eyes and try to sniff back the tears.

He observes me silently for a moment. 'Oh, Ella, that's where you're wrong. When I told you that you were special, I meant it. You are the first person I've ever met whose entire consciousness has transferred over wholesale, the first person for whom I've been able to piece together a full explanation for what's occurred. But, most of all, you are special because you can help me to prove my theory. Why? Because I know you – I work at your college – in both universes. I asked the others to contact me when they returned to their other universes, but they either forgot me during the journey, or couldn't find me. You, however, will be able to tell me yourself that I was right.'

You *will* be able to tell me. That's what he said. So my fate is decided then, in his mind, at least: I'm going to die.

But I don't want to die.

'I've got to go,' I say, jumping up from the bed again. 'I need some fresh air.' I stumble to the door, scared that he might come after me and try to stop me, scared too that if he thinks I won't go through with his plan, he might try to kill me himself.

'Ella . . . Wait. Don't run away. Don't be frightened. We need to talk this through.' He tries to clamber up to follow me, but he's been sitting cross-legged on the floor for too long, and he's stiff and slow. By the time he is standing up straight, I have undone the latch and found my way out into the hall. I take the stairs two at a time, and I don't pause for breath until I have burst out through the front door and I am standing outside in the street.

26

Will

I know now that I have to make a horrible, impossible choice, and it is no choice at all. For me, there is either death or this untenable half life, which isn't a life, which is barely an existence. I can choose a violent and painful end, or I can accept that I will be stuck here forever, in a world where I am not fully me and will never be me. Or worse, entirely gone. Does dying hurt more than living? Who can tell me that? I start to take my phone out of my bag so that I can call someone, but then I realise there's no one to call, and I don't want to talk about it any more. I don't want to think any more. All I want is to be held; to know that I am alive; to hear the sound of someone else breathing; to sense their skin on my skin; to fill the void inside me. All I want is Will.

I am at his house within minutes. Praying that he's in tonight, I text him, asking him to come to the front door. A light comes on in the hall and I see a flicker of movement through the glass. The door opens. 'This is a surprise!' he

232

says, leaning over to kiss my cheek. I'm lucky he doesn't remember that he's never given me his address. His hair is wet, as if he's just got out of the shower after football training.

'Yeah,' I say. 'Are your parents around? Your brother?'

He shakes his head. 'No, I've got the place to myself.'

'Good,' I say. 'Let's go to your bedroom.' I take his hand and steer him towards the stairs, before I can change my mind. I feel more nervous than I anticipated. I don't think I've ever been this forward before.

'OK,' he says, allowing himself to be led. He looks surprised, but he doesn't object. At the top of the stairs, he stops. 'It's a bit of a mess, my room,' he says, embarrassed. 'I didn't know you were coming.'

I laugh. Billy's room was always a mess. 'It doesn't matter.'

He opens the door and even before we are properly inside I am grasping at his face and pulling it down towards mine, my lips hungry for his lips, my tongue greedy for his tongue. His hands paw at my jacket and he swings me round and up against the wall, kicking the door shut with his foot. 'Lock it,' I whisper. Mouths glued together, arms wrapped tightly around each other, we circle the room in a kind of jerky dance, until I catch the side of his bed with my knee and, unbalanced, we tumble on to it, rolling our way into the middle. We come to rest with me on top of him, his belt buckle digging into my tummy and, beneath it, something hard and hot pressed tight against my leg. Instinctively, I rub myself against his body, feeling like I'm going to explode with excitement and desire, breathing so fast that I grow dizzy. My fingers begin to fumble for his shirt buttons, and for his belt. Then, suddenly, unexpectedly, his hand is on my shoulder, gently pushing me away.

'Ella, stop a second. Please.' He rolls out from under me. 'Wait.'

I sit up, lean back against the wall and self-consciously smooth down my hair. 'What's wrong? Don't you have anything?'

'It's not that,' he says, and I notice that he is trembling. 'I do. In the drawer by the bed. I'm just . . . I . . .'

He doesn't need to say it; I already know: he's a virgin. Of course he is – because this is Will, not Billy, and in this universe he didn't meet me at thirteen. In this universe, we've never done it in a car, or locked ourselves in the bathroom at his mate Andy's party and done it, drunkenly and clumsily and uncomfortably, while somebody banged on the door outside. In this universe, he's been too busy playing football to have a girlfriend. This is his very first time. Right here. Right now. With the new me.

'It's OK,' I say, kissing him on his forehead, on his cheeks, on his neck, with tender, butterfly kisses. 'It's not a problem. I don't care.' We find each other's mouths again and we kiss more gently than before, as if now it really means something.

'But . . .' He stops me again. 'Aren't you? I mean, have you ever . . .?'

I stiffen. I have no idea how to answer him. 'No . . . Yes . . . Er, I dunno.'

He strokes my face, laughing. 'How can you not know whether you're a virgin?'

How about because I really don't? In my mind, I am not a virgin. In my memory, I am not a virgin. But is my body? This body? In this universe? I'm not certain. I know only what my friends have told me, that I have never done more than kiss a boy. 'I've fooled around a bit,' I say, thinking quickly. 'And, sometimes, well, it's a bit of a blurry line. But it was another life, you know?'

To my relief, that seems to be enough of an explanation for him. I guess he doesn't want to waste time talking, any more than I do. He starts to kiss me again, and we find ourselves lying back across his unmade bed, and somehow this time he ends up on top of me. I gasp as he slides his hand inside my jeans, moaning softly as his fingers work their way into my knickers. He traces my pubic hair with his fingertips, but he doesn't say anything about me not shaving, doesn't act like it's disgusting, and I think, gratefully, that perhaps Will doesn't watch as much porn as Billy did. Soon we are wriggling out of our clothes and I have to take off my own bra because he can't manage to undo the clasp. I make sure that this time I pull my socks off before I forget, tossing them on to the floor. And then we are giggling because he can't open the condom or put it on either, and he's complaining that it's too small, which it isn't (although I don't say that), so I have to help him. And then instinct takes over and my legs are further apart than I think they can go, and at last he is pushing himself into me – and it does hurt, just a little bit, like my other first time did, but it feels good too, and right. As he moves inside me, I open my eyes and I recognise the look on his face, his gaze slightly unfocused, his expression

235

one of intense concentration. For one wonderful moment, I forget everything that has happened to me and I feel whole again. There is only one universe, one Ella, one me. Then he shudders and makes the same deep grunting sound that Billy always did, and it's over. And I am back in a messy bedroom, with a boy I barely know, and a slightly sore feeling inside me.

Perhaps, as Daniel said, some things really are destined to happen in every universe. This must be one of them. The circumstances may differ, but Billy and Ella, Will and Ella, we will always be each other's first.

27

Making a Decision

A few months ago, when I was me, properly me, I had a life. It wasn't a perfect life, or a particularly exciting life, but it was a life that I didn't question: my life. I knew who I was and where I was going; I knew my tastes, who my friends were, who I liked and disliked, and how they felt about me too. I'd learned who I could trust and who to avoid; I had a clear idea of what the future held.

And then I woke up and found myself trapped in this higgledy-piggledy universe, where nothing is as it should be. Here, I have friends who I don't know and can't relate to – and who I suspect don't even like the real me all that much – plus a former best friend who thinks I'm a stalker. Here, I have parents who have stupidly stayed together, when they'd be so much happier apart and, in my dad's case, still happier again if he'd only meet a lonely lady who comes into the cafe where I work. I may have the same boyfriend, and although he is sweet and gorgeous and too much in lust with me to have hurt me yet, I know that he soon will; it's inevitable. My college grades are slipping and I can't even be bothered to try to fake it any more. The fact is that I am stuck on a path I don't remember choosing and now can't divert from. Even if I wanted to, I can't live up to the other me. It's only a matter of time before I fail and I disappoint, before everything falls apart. Although I didn't always like the old me, at least she was real, her life the result of choices and mistakes I made willingly, and that I can remember making.

So what, truly, is keeping me here? What, apart from the fear of dying? I've been mulling it over for days and days and, so far, that's the only compelling reason I can come up with. That, and not liking pain very much. Of course, going back has consequences too. For one thing, it means I'll be 'killing' the old lady, although I know that she will still be alive here. It also means returning to a world where there are nude images of me online, but I'm certain I'm strong enough to deal with that now. One of the few positives I can take from being here is that I've learned I can stand up to Will – and, therefore, to Billy – without losing him. I've learned I can do more with my time than just hang out with my boyfriend and mates too. Once I'm back, I can get myself another Saturday job, if I want. Hey, maybe there's even a vacancy in the same cafe in the other universe.

If I sound blasé, it's only because I have done enough crying over the past few days for several lifetimes in any number of universes. I've been over and over the same things, torturing myself, always reaching the same conclusion. And now I'm numb with it all. I wonder if all the others went through this too, if they had similar thought processes before they made their terrible, final choice. Shame I can't ask them. Shame I can't discuss this with anybody.

I've bunked off college all week, spending my days in parks and cafes and libraries, and I've barely seen or spoken to a soul. Even the old lady has eluded me. As a result, I'm starting to get concerned text messages from friends, which I am doing my best to ignore. *Are you ill again, Ella? Has something happened? Call me, Ella, I'm worried.* Daniel has texted me too. I didn't turn up for my last tutorial session; I've been avoiding him, for obvious reasons. The problem is I'm now becoming quite desperate to speak to him. I can't move forward without knowing all the facts and I need to know exactly how he thinks I will be able to prove his theory.

So, after a lot of thought, I agree to go to my next session, this Friday. I'm not scared of him any more. What can he do to me in a classroom, even if there aren't that many people around after college hours? More to the point, what can he possibly do to me that's worse than what I'm contemplating doing to myself?

He looks relieved when he sees me, a fleeting smile crossing his lips. 'You've made the right choice coming back,' he says. 'You shouldn't have run away from me last week, or ignored my texts. I sincerely hope you haven't told anyone that you came to my flat.'

'I didn't, OK? The guy in the kebab shop might have seen me, but that's all. And I don't think he'll say anything.'

'Even your boyfriend?'

'Especially not my boyfriend.' Will is the last person I'd tell. Not only would he not understand any of this in a million light years, I also know how jealous he gets. And he's twice the size of Daniel. 'Look, I've got no intention of telling on you to anyone.'

'Good,' he says. 'Well, now we've got that out of the way, I'm very glad you've come today. For what it's worth, I think I owe you an apology. I'm sorry about the way you found everything out. It wasn't meant to happen like that and I didn't mean to freak you out. I'm a scientist, but I'm not too clever when it comes to the touchy-feely emotional stuff, you know? I am generally much better with atoms and neutrons than humans.'

I laugh. 'Too right, Mr Spock. Apology accepted.'

'But you absolutely shouldn't be dealing with this alone. So please let me help you now.'

I shrug. 'Help me how? To top myself? Gee, thanks.'

'No, Ella. Help you to go home safely, to the universe where you belong, if that's what you want. But if you don't want that, if you've changed your mind and have decided you are happy to remain here, then I will accept it. I won't say another word about multiverses and we can just go back to studying the syllabus every week.'

I roll my eyes. We both know that's not going to happen.

'Your life. Your choice.'

'Lives,' I say, emphasising the 's'. 'My lives. Anyway, you said they might switch me off back in my other life, and then my brain would explode here. So it doesn't seem like I have much of a choice.'

He nods. 'That is a possibility. Although I don't think your brain would explode. It would be more like an implosion, a sudden shutting down of your consciousness.'

'Yeah, well, whatever. I'd end up dead or some sort of vegetable.'

'Potentially.'

'So let's cut the bullshit. How do I do it then?' I can't bring myself to say 'kill myself'. Maybe because, in my eyes, that's not what I'll be doing. 'Do I get instructions?'

'It's up to you. The most important thing is that you succeed, and that you don't totally obliterate your brain matter. If that happens, you could be trapped between the two universes forever.'

'Oh damn, so I can't blow my brains out with my handy gun then?'

He doesn't smile. 'That isn't funny, Ella. This subject really isn't funny.'

'Haven't you heard of black humour, Daniel? It's the only way to get through it without cracking up. Or do you only know about black holes?' He bristles. I know I'm being rude but I can't help myself, and standing up to him feels good.

'You seem very detached. Not like yourself at all.'

'Which self is that then? Honestly, how do you expect me to be? Would you rather I was crying like a little girl?'

He doesn't answer me; he just shakes his head. Eventually, he says: 'This is a leap of faith for both of us, a journey into the unknown. I wasn't there for the others but I do want to be there for you.'

241

'You mean you want to be with me when I do it? That would be good. I'd rather not be alone.'

'You know that's not possible, Ella. I can't be there with you, or implicated in your decision or your actions, not in any way. That's why it's essential your phone is clear of my number, and of any messages between us. But I can help you prepare, and try to help make it as painless as possible.'

So I am alone with this, just as I have been alone since the morning I woke up in my alien bedroom. What was it that Daniel said, under his breath, the first time we met? *Oh, but we are all on our own.*

He stands up and reaches into his pocket, pulling out a small foil strip containing two tiny pills. I have no idea what they are; they look like proper medicine, not street drugs. 'When you have decided and are ready to do it, take these.' He leans over to give me the strip. 'They won't cloud your judgement but they will make you feel relaxed and take the edge off your fear.'

'Um, thank you,' I say, putting the strip away in my bag. 'So let's say that I do go ahead, theoretically. I still don't understand how you will know that it's worked. How can I communicate with you from my other life, across the universes, to prove I'm back? Have you got some sort of cosmic megaphone?'

He laughs. 'If only. But we don't need one. You're forgetting that I'll be there in your other universe too – at this college, working in the labs. I won't know you, of course, because you won't be studying sciences, and I certainly won't be your tutor; I will only have seen you in passing. But you will know me, and you will remember everything we have discussed here. You will be able to tell me the whole story. And, to provide cast-iron proof so that I believe you, I am going to give you a message, which I need you to memorise. It is something that nobody else knows about me, something that you couldn't possibly know unless I had told you. When you go back, and you are ready and able, you are going to come to see me. As soon as you tell me this message, I will know that you have successfully jumped universes and that my theory is correct.'

'But what if I forget to do it or I just can't remember the message?'

'It's a risk we'll have to take. I hope to God that you won't.'

'So this message, what is it? Can't it be something simple like, um, "There's no place like home?"'

'Too generic,' he says. 'It has to be personal to me, something nobody else could guess, something you couldn't come up with on your own. I have been thinking about this, over the past few days, and I think I have it . . .' He moves towards me, coming closer than is comfortable. 'I'm going to whisper it to you; we cannot risk anyone else hearing. It is not something that I want to get out.'

'OK.' He leans in to me and I feel his breath tingle in my ear. What he has to say makes me shudder and recoil. Part of it I don't understand, but it's easy enough to remember. It's not the sort of thing you'd forget.

'Repeat it to yourself over and over until it sticks,' he says. 'They might just be the most important words you will ever speak.'

243

28

An Intervention

I leave soon after that, aware that we have come to the natural end of our tutoring sessions and that I will probably not see Daniel again, not in this universe, anyway. Any communication between us from now on will be done by erasable text message. I'm glad about that; he really is too weird. The bus doesn't come and so I walk most of the way home, with an empty end-of-term type feeling, thinking about what I must do, and how.

It comes to me when I am halfway up the hill, just a few streets from my house: the ideal place, the perfect way to make my 'leap of faith'. It's so obvious, I'm surprised it hadn't occurred to me before. I smile to myself, feeling curiously calmer than I have in weeks.

When I open my front door I can hear voices coming from the kitchen, too many voices to belong to Mum and Dad alone. At first I wonder if my parents are entertaining friends, but they haven't done that together since I was a kid. I'm not in the mood to be sociable, so I try to sneak straight up the stairs to my room without being seen or heard. It doesn't work.

'Ella! Is that you?' calls Mum. 'Come into the kitchen, darling. There's some people here to see you.'

I stop halfway up the stairs, and grimace. 'Do I have to? I'm tired. I just want to go to my room and lie down before dinner.'

'Yes, Ella, you do. Come down here, please.'

Reluctantly, I do as she says. The sight that greets me is the last thing I am expecting: Mum is sitting at the kitchen table with Rachel and Jen and Dom. They're all having cups of tea and biscuits, like it's the most normal thing in the world. I stand by the door, open-mouthed, wondering what the hell is going on. Perhaps I've slipped into yet another universe, or down a rabbit hole and have found myself at the Mad Hatter's Tea Party.

'Right,' says Mum. 'I'll leave you young people to it then. I'll be upstairs if you need anything.'

My friends murmur their heartfelt appreciation for my mother's extreme generosity, as though tea and milk-chocolate Digestives are as expensive and rare as the finest champagne and caviar, and then Rachel gets up and comes over to give me a hug. I just stand there, letting her, my arms hanging limply by my sides. 'What on earth are you all doing here? Together? Is it someone's birthday or something?'

'Come and sit down,' says Dom. 'Do you want some tea?'

'No thank you. Just tell me what's going on.'

'We were worried,' says Jen. 'You didn't turn up at college, didn't reply to our messages, and nobody knew what was going on with you. We thought, at first, that maybe you were just being off with us – with me and Rachel. But then Dom called us and said he was worried too, and so we asked Will, and he said he thought you were fine, but he hadn't seen you since last week. So we figured we'd better all come round to make sure you're OK.'

'Jeez. Is Will coming too?'

'No,' says Dom. 'He's got football practice.' He sneers. 'He said he'd call you later.'

At least someone is behaving normally. 'Thank God for that. Well, you can all see that I'm absolutely fine,' I lie, not very convincingly. 'I'm really sorry I ignored your texts – that's my bad. I had some thinking to do, some stuff to sort out. I didn't have another accident, or bang my head again, or anything like that. So please just go now. I don't want to break up your lovely little tea party, but I need some space. I want to be on my own. I promise I won't ignore you all again.'

'We're not going anywhere yet,' says Rachel. 'And don't think being mean to us will work.'

'I'm not being mean. Honestly, I just need to lie down – I've got a headache. We can talk another time.'

Rachel isn't quitting. 'Dom has told us about Mr Perry. We can't just leave it.'

'What about Mr Perry?'

'He filled us in on when you met at the British Museum,' says Jen. 'Don't worry, I'm not angry at you for meeting him or anything. I'm over all that. He told us what you said about Mr Perry, about how weird you sounded, not like you at all. All that parallel-universe bollocks. He thinks you've been brainwashed.'

'You've got it wrong. Mr Perry – Daniel – is the only one who understands what I've been going through the past few months. You've all said it yourself – I seem different – but you've assumed it's just because of my accident and won't even consider that there might be something bigger going on. Yes, Daniel is a bit, er, odd, creepy even, but he is not what you're making him out to be. He's not some evil cult leader. And I'm perfectly capable of thinking for myself.'

'So you don't believe you're in a parallel universe?'

I hesitate. If I say yes, they'll have me down as a poor, brainwashed victim. It's best to lie. 'Of course I don't. I was just saying how I felt, you know, like, metaphorically. I'm afraid Dom got the wrong end of the stick.'

Dom doesn't seem convinced. 'That's not what you said at the time. Anyway, it's not normal, Ella, the amount of time you've been spending with him. What do you talk about?'

'He's my maths and science tutor. We talk about atoms and equations.'

'Then why,' says Jen, 'are your grades going down, not up?'

I don't have an answer for that.

'We're going to report him,' says Rachel. 'Sorry, but it all seems really dodgy. We just want our friend back and he's making you worse, not better. The college should know.'

'Report him for what? Me not doing my homework?'

'For inappropriate behaviour. We're going to see the principal first thing on Monday.'

I shake my head with frustration. 'You have no idea what you're talking about, or what you're doing. Just leave it, OK? I'm not having any more sessions with him anyway, so you don't need to waste your energy. Everything's sorted and I'm going to be fine. Very soon, you won't have to worry about me any more.'

'What do you mean?' says Dom. 'You're not planning on doing anything stupid, are you?'

I shouldn't have said that. I smile. 'No, nothing stupid. So can you all please go? It's lovely that you care but I don't need this right now. Next time I see you I'll be much happier. A totally different person, in fact.'

It takes a lot more persuading to get them to leave, but they go eventually. At the front door, I give each of them an extra-special hug, a goodbye hug, although I hope they can't tell it's that. I reserve the biggest, squishiest, most special hug of all for Dom, who I know I probably won't see again once I arrive 'home' to my original life. Rachel and Jen I'll pass in the corridors at college. I might even try to befriend them. But Dom? I won't come across him, not unless I seek him out.

Much to their surprise, I hug Mum and Dad too before I go to bed. I chat to Will and enjoy his mushy declarations of love. I even tell him that I love him too. And then I text Daniel.

I've made a decision. I'm going to do it tomorrow. So I guess this is goodbye.

29

A Leap of Faith

I pause to catch my breath, putting down my rucksack. So many steps; I stopped counting at forty. I am at the top now, almost at my destination. London spreads out before me like a model village: toy-sized houses and parks and office blocks as far as the eye can see, out to the river and the Eye, the Gherkin and the Shard. They glint in the sun, like a perfect postcard image. It almost seems a shame not to take a photograph.

Twenty metres high. That's a long way down. That's ten tall men, standing straight on top of each other, feet to head, feet to head. I've passed under this bridge so many times throughout my life, on foot, on the bus, in my parents' cars. But I've never climbed up here before, scarcely even gazed up at it. Suicide Bridge, they call it. That's why I picked it. That's why the railings are so high, and why there are spikes on the top. It could almost be funny, but I think now that I'm a little bit more afraid of heights than I realised. I've been concentrating so hard on what happens afterwards, when it's done, that I haven't considered what it will be like to do it. How will it feel to fly, to fall? Will it be like the sensation I have experienced in my dreams – plummeting like a stone, my insides turning over and over? This is going to be so much harder than I imagined.

I swallow twice, trying to quell my nerves. The pills that Daniel gave me have taken the edge off my fear but I am still terrified, my mouth dry and my heart thumping. I dare myself to look down, through the gaps in the railings. On the pavements on either side of the bridge there are tiny matchstick figures, a boy and a girl holding hands, a man with a dog, a woman pushing a shopping trolley. It might even be the old woman, real or ghostly, here to witness the end of our story. I can see the cars beneath me, brightly coloured metal boxes, whooshing along like waves. Occasionally, they slow or stop and I catch a glimpse of a face, or a flash of hands on a steering wheel. Not one of them looks up to see me. Not one of them has a clue that in a few minutes I will be a missile, hurtling towards them. Better not to think of them as people. Better not to think of them at all.

I can hear police sirens in the distance. Someone may have reported seeing a girl standing still for too long on the bridge, guessed my intentions. Or perhaps the sirens aren't for me at all. I let my imagination roam, self-indulgently, and picture Daniel and Dom here, each standing at opposite sides of the bridge, one encouraging me to jump, the other pleading with me to stop. Daniel's reply to my text last night was characteristically brief and cold: *I wish you a safe journey*, he had said, as if I was catching the train to Birmingham. I can't remember if I deleted it or not.

It is almost time. I kick my rucksack to the side, for someone to find later. There is a note inside, explaining everything, but I know nobody will believe what I have written. They'll dismiss it, saying I was ill or depressed, or being manipulated, that I haven't been right in the head for months. But that doesn't matter because I won't hear them; I'll be somewhere else, somewhere better. Or nowhere at all.

Using all the strength in my arms, I clamber up the railings and hoist myself on to the base of the lamp post, which marks the centre of the bridge. The spikes get caught in my jeans, ripping a hole, grazing my leg. I don't feel it. It's windy up here and I'm scared I'll fall before I'm ready. I try to balance myself, wrapping my arms around the lamp post in a tight hug, and I stand still for a moment, looking out at the clouds. I follow the wispy white trail of an aeroplane until it dissolves into sky, and then I shut my eyes.

The sirens are growing closer, my heart beating so fast that I feel dizzy. I have only seconds to make my decision: jump or climb down. Stay or go. Remain trapped here forever or be free.

What if Daniel is wrong? What if it doesn't work? What if he's lying?

I don't want to die; I want to live.

I want to be me again.

30 (a)

Afterwards

I am waking up in a hospital bed, in a sterile room, to the sound of machines rhythmically beeping. I choke as I try to breathe, struggling against whatever it is that's blocking my throat, panicking and crying voicelessly for help. The beeping intensifies, becoming frantic, and then there is a commotion all around me, as doctors and nurses swoop to my bed. Something is wrenched from my throat and suddenly I am gulping cool, fresh air, coughing and swallowing painfully, but breathing for myself. When I try to speak, my voice is nothing but a croak.

'What's that she's saying?' It's my mother's voice. I force open my eyes, blinking against the bright lights. Even though my vision is blurry, I can see that her hair is chestnut brown, although her roots need doing.

'I'm not sure,' says an unknown voice. 'Something about home?'

I try again, but my lips are so dry that they're sticking to my teeth. Someone pushes a straw into my mouth. I suck at it greedily, most of the water dribbling out down my chin. It's hard to control my tongue or my lips.

'I think she's saying "There's no place like home",' says Mum. 'She always loved *The Wizard of Oz*.' I feel her take my hand and stroke it, and I smile.

The next few days blur into one. Most of the time I am asleep, dreaming of strange worlds where I don't belong, of friends who don't know me and parents who are still together. Sometimes I awake to find visitors in my room, usually my mum or dad, or Deeta. Billy comes once, but doesn't stay long. Everyone brings gifts of fruit and chocolates, and Deeta brings a Louise Brooks DVD. On the third day, I feel strong enough to sit up in bed and chat.

'Would you have switched me off, Mum?' I ask. 'If I'd stayed in the coma for too much longer?'

'Of course not, darling. We always knew that you'd come out of it eventually. The doctors couldn't find a reason for your coma – they said your brain activity was very unusual.'

'But if the doctors had said there was no more hope?'

'We wouldn't have listened to them. I promise.'

I smile. 'Thanks. How did I end up in hospital? I don't remember anything. What happened to me?'

'You were in a car accident. Billy was giving you a driving lesson and you lost control of the car.'

'I was driving?' I hesitate, feeling sick, not wanting to know the answer to my next question. 'Did I kill an old lady?'

'Kill an old lady?' says Mum. She laughs nervously. 'Wherever did you get that idea? No, it was just a fox that ran into the road.'

I start to cry uncontrollably, first out of sheer relief and then out of guilt at my relief. 'Poor, poor fox.'

'Oh, Ella,' Mum says. 'Don't get upset. It was only a mangy old fox. It shouldn't have been there.'

Later, Dad comes to visit me with Tamsyn. They're so obviously happy together, and Tamsyn seems genuinely pleased that I'm awake. I keep smiling at her, because I want her to know that I'm aware she's not all that bad, underneath the wicked stepmother facade. She looks bemused.

'I know this is a random question but there's something I wanted to ask you both. I don't think you ever told me. Where exactly did you meet?'

'Why on earth do you want to hear about that now?' says Dad. 'But if you must know, it was in a cafe on the high street, one Saturday afternoon.'

I am in hospital for a few more weeks, just for observation the doctors say. They don't understand my coma, or my sudden miraculous recovery, and they want to make sure it is safe to send me home. A week later, bored and lonely, I decide I'm ready to go back to college. I have missed several months of work, but I turn down the offer of extra tuition. I'm sure that, with Deeta's help, I can catch up.

At the end of my first day back, Deeta suggests we go for a coffee to celebrate.

'There's something I need to do first,' I tell her. 'You go. I'll meet you in Costa. I won't be long.'

Most people have gone home, and the college is quiet. I walk down the corridors towards the science department, hoping that I'll be in time to catch him before he leaves.

I've known I have to do this ever since I left hospital; there's no point putting it off. I stop at room 123 and knock on the door.

A familiar voice says: 'Enter.'

I walk into the room. Daniel looks just the same, just as odd and wiry as I remember. 'Excuse me, Mr Perry? Daniel?'

He stares at me. 'Do I know you? How do you know my first name?'

'Because you told me. You won't remember. Anyway, I've got a message for you and I've travelled a hell of a long way to bring it to you.'

'Message? Who from?' A crooked smile begins to form at the corners of his mouth, as if he somehow knows what the message might be. 'Go on . . . Tell me . . .'

I clear my throat. 'Your theory is right: we can jump universes. And I am proof of that.'

He hops from foot to foot, more excited than I've ever seen him. 'How do I know that this isn't a wind-up?'

'You predicted that you would think that when I came to tell you. That's why, in the other universe, you told me a secret that nobody knows but me, something you've never told a soul.'

'Ah, insurance. That was clever of me. Go on . . .'

I cringe at the thought of what I'm about to say. It still creeps me out. 'OK. When you were ten, you killed Brandy, the family cat. You put him in a box, so you could try to prove Schrödinger's paradox theory that a cat can be both dead and alive at the same time. But there weren't any air holes and the cat suffocated. You waited until everyone was asleep and then buried it in the back garden. To this day, your parents think the cat ran away.'

The colour has drained from his face. 'How on earth could you possibly know that?'

'I told you how: because you told me. In another universe, just before I took a leap of faith and jumped off a bridge. I'm Ella, by the way. Ella Samson.'

'Thank you, Ella,' he says. 'Thank you. Thank you. You have no idea how much this means to me.' He starts moving towards me, as if he's going to hug me. I shudder and take a step back. Now that I've kept my promise, I don't want to have anything more to do with him. Not if I can help it.

'Oh but I do,' I say. 'I really do. Now please excuse me, but I have to go. I haven't been back long and, well, now that I'm me again, I've got a life I need to live.'

30 (b)

Afterwards

And in another universe, I am not waking up at all. My bedroom is empty, my bed still freshly made, my possessions exactly where I left them. This isn't a bedroom any more, it's a storage cupboard for possessions that will slowly date and fade, a shrine. It's a place where my mother will come to cry, and a room that my father will not be able to bring himself to enter. There will be more arguments than ever leaking through its walls, more anger and recriminations, guilt and blame, but I will not be able to hear them. This room will not be touched for a year or two until, with the inevitable divorce, the house will be sold and my personal effects packed up into boxes, and moved somewhere else. Some of them will end up in the local charity shops.

Next week, on a cold and rainy Thursday, they will be holding my funeral. It will be very well attended, with half the college there, mostly people who'll claim they were my friends but who never actually spoke to me. Even Deeta will come along to show her support. She'll cry her eyeliner off, telling everyone how she wishes she had reported my weird behaviour, how she should have been more sympathetic to me, but she hadn't known I'd needed help. And her friends will hug her and say, 'It's not your fault; you weren't to know she was ill. There was nothing you could do to stop her jumping.' Will will be devastated, but he won't talk to anyone about it; he'll just kick footballs, and walls, and people. Jen and Rachel and Dom will find comfort in each other and, in a month or two, Jen and Dom will discover that from all that shared grief a deeper connection has grown, and their hugs will turn to passionate kisses.

The inquest will say I was depressed and confused following a head injury, that nobody can be sure I meant to jump. They'll cite all the websites I looked at, with stories of random suicides, all over the country. There will be a short news story about my death in the local newspaper, and I'll be mentioned again as part of the ongoing campaign to make the bridge safer. Someone will start a Facebook tribute page for me and lots of people will post lovely messages, before all the trolls come out from their dark hiding places to insult me. After a while, nobody will post anything on the page at all. At college I'll become the poster child for depression and alienation, and there will be a spate of copycat suicide attempts and self-harm incidents. Someone from a mental health charity will come to give a talk, after which posters with helpline numbers will appear on every noticeboard.

Daniel will be investigated for inappropriate conduct with a student and, ultimately, will lose his job at the college, but he won't be prosecuted, owing to lack of evidence. A text message wishing someone a pleasant journey doesn't, after all, constitute assisting someone's suicide. He will continue his PhD from his bedsit, supplementing his income by working in the kebab shop downstairs.

And, every so often, he will think of me and wonder if, in another universe, where he still has a job as a lab technician at a sixth-form college, I have come to find him and proved his theory right.

30 (c)

Afterwards

And in yet another universe, I am waking up in a recently painted room, in a bed that's been pushed up against the wall. It is the same room I woke up in yesterday morning and, I daresay, I will be waking up here again tomorrow, and the next day, and the next. My white-haired mother is downstairs in the kitchen and my father is pottering around in the spare room. They are avoiding each other.

I came so close, so close, but I didn't jump yesterday. I climbed down from my diving post at the top of Suicide Bridge and, legs trembling, walked right back down the stairs I'd just climbed up. I wish I could say it's because I changed my mind, or came to my senses, or realised just how great this universe really is, but I can't. The only reason I didn't jump is because I was too chicken. If I could have leaped into my preferred universe without splattering myself all over the road, without the dying part, I would have done it in a flash. No question. Instead,

I'm going to have to do it the hard way; changing things little by little.

After my initial relief at not dying had passed, I felt angry with myself for losing my nerve. But then I started to think. Even if Daniel's theory is correct, who's to say that I'd have ended up in the right universe – in the one I wanted to be in? I might have found myself somewhere worse than here, having to start all over again. What's that expression? Better the devil you know.

I texted Daniel last night, telling him I hadn't been able to go through with it, and warning him that my friends are planning to report him to the college authorities tomorrow morning – and that I'm not sure I can stop them. He hasn't replied yet. He's probably sitting in his bedsit destroying evidence, hoping that someone switches the other me off, so that my brain explodes before the principal summons him to her office.

Those sirens I heard from the bridge weren't for me. I guess there are plenty of other emergencies in North London on a Saturday morning. Nobody knows that I was planning to jump, and I'd prefer to keep it that way. It's going to be hard enough to persuade Rachel and Jen and Dom that I am sane, and neither depressed nor brainwashed. I suppose I'm going to have to make more of an effort with them, now that I've decided to stay. They've proved how much they really care and, let's face it, I don't have a surfeit of friends to choose from. They probably deserve far better than me.

This is who I am now.

My name is Ella Samson. I am seventeen years and six months old. An only child, I live with my bickering parents in a small house in North London. I have a boyfriend called Will and two best friends called Rachel and Jen. I was seeing a guy called Dom, but that's complicated, and now he's just a mate. I have a Saturday job in a cafe, volunteer at a children's hospice and I'm hoping to become an architect. I'm also a huge fan of the silent movie star Louise Brooks. There isn't much else to tell. I like music and art and watching films. And, it turns out, I've got a phobia of heights.

It's not a particularly exciting life, but it's my life.

And I'm bloody well going to try my best to live it.

Acknowledgements

Thank you to my agent Catherine Pellegrino and to my editor and publisher, Brenda Gardner, and the teams at both Piccadilly Press and Hot Key Books. A special mention should go to Melissa Hyder and Shane Hegarty, whose science-fiction knowledge and explanatory diagrams were so invaluable at the start (and saved me a lot of brain-ache).

Thanks again to Janine and Mark, the Garai-Ebners, who bid in the 2013 Authors for the Philippines auction, winning the chance to have their children's names immortalised in my next book. That's why my two main characters in this book are named Ella and Daniel.

Many thanks to Dr Carol Cooper for the medical advice, and to Professor Brian Cowan for the lesson in quantum physics.

A huge thank you to the generous support of the Royal Literary Fund and to Arts Council England for a lottery-funded Buying Time to Write grant, without which this book would never have been written.

And an enormous debt of gratitude is owed to my friends and fellow writers Keren David and Caroline Green, who acted as my readers and gave me so much support and encouragement. Not to forget the wonderful YA Thinkers who helped (when they weren't distracting me) so much with the writing process. Finally, thank you to all my friends and family for being there, *et merci beaucoup et gros bisous* to my partner, Mickael Lorinquer, for his love and patience, and for giving up his daily baguette in the sunshine.